BRANCH SHIPMENTS

ARC
B.L.
FER
FOR
GAR
HOA
K-T
McK
R.D.
TRN
BKM

WYOMING WAY

Dan Ruylander led his Rafter R crew to Oregon to purchase a herd of cattle. He also went to exact revenge on Owen Terrill's Triangle T brand for a wrong Dan's father had suffered thirty years ago. Owen was dead now, but his son Garry ran the Triangle with brutal ramrod Hawk Fallon.

Bad blood rose quickly between the Rafter and Triangle men, but Dan still allowed Garry and his crew to join the drive back to Wyoming. Then to complicate his plans further, Dan fell hard for the lovely Sue Terrill, Garry's sister.

Ahead lay a thousand-mile trek. And with one eye on Garry Terrill and one eye on Fallon, who itched to put him in his grave—Dan knew he might never reach the Rafter again. But he had promised his father he'd see this deal through—even if the price was his own life!

WYOMING WAY

Roe Richmond

GUNSMOKE

WESTERNS

First published by Avalon Books

This hardback edition 1995
by Chivers Press
by arrangement with Golden West Literary Agency

ISBN 0 7451 4662 7

British Library Cataloguing in Publication Data available

Printed and bound in Great Britain by
Redwood Books, Trowbridge, Wiltshire

For Evelyn *and* Fritz;
in memory of Dad *and* Mom,
Ken *and* Ruth

One

It had started thirty years ago in 1851, six years before Dan was born. It was his father Dirk's story, but Dan knew it as if he had lived it himself. At times it seemed more real than the reality of the present. At others it was like pure fantasy. No matter what, the long-delayed conclusion would be on his shoulders. He accepted this with a strange mixture of pride and resentment.

Dan Ruylander crossed the lobby of the Inter-Ocean Hotel in Cheyenne, the smoke of an after-breakfast cigarette pleasant in his mouth. Spring sunshine striped the heavy elegance of the furnishings, and Dan felt a trifle stiff and dressed-up in his tailored traveling suit, white shirt and black string tie. Older men nodded and spoke to him, absently and out of deference to his father, and Dan responded with quiet shyness. Wyoming ranchers, bankers, businessmen, and dignitaries of the Territorial government all respected Derek Ruylander of Rafter R.

On the shaded porch old Jud Crater lounged against the rail beside a tangled mound of warbags, saddle gear and carbines, chewing tobacco and squinting into the morning brilliance, a bit uncomfortable in his rusty store suit. A thin whip of a man with a tough seamed face of brown leather, pale-eyed and acid-mouthed, he spoke in a gravel rasp:

"Dirk's at the club, Danny. Better dig the boys outa Magill's and send 'em over. I ain't toting this stuff to the station for nobody."

"I'll get 'em, Jud. Nice day for it."

Crater cuffed the hat back on his gray head. "Helluva day to be boarding a goddamn train. Oughta make old Dirk go himself. His idea, Dan."

Dan Ruylander nodded in grave understanding. He wasn't too happy about this trip himself, and Jud had a right to criticize Dirk Ruylander. They had been together over a quarter of a century, for more years than Dan had been alive. "See some country, Jud," he said.

"I saw it last year, son."

"Well, you can show it to us."

Jud Crater squirted an amber stream across the railing. "Guardeen for five wild-eyed young broncs. I sure draw the goddamn details. Better drift, Dan. Only got about an hour."

Walking along the street Dan was thoughtful. Thirty years ago in 1851, the wagons had rolled west and north from the Mississippi, up the Missouri to Independence and Fort Kearney. Up the North Platte toward Scott's Bluff and Fort Laramie and the great plains of Wyoming. Ox-drawn hulks under bleached canvas wallowing through dust and heat on creaking wheels and groaning axles. The wreckage and castoff gear, the graves and whitened bones of earlier emigrant trains marking the way. The slow miles took their toll and the caravan left its own dead in places, along with the bloating carcasses of oxen and mules . . . . Derek Ruylander had come west with this company from Pennsylvania, bound for faraway Oregon. A big blond smiling man in the prime of life.

But Dirk had never gone beyond Fort Laramie with that expedition in '51, which was the reason for sending his son Dan to Oregon in this springtime of 1881. With

6

Jud Crater and four other riders, to drive home a herd of Durhams and Herefords.

Dan Ruylander turned into Magill's and the smell of beer and sawdust and tobacco, with ivory balls clicking on the pool tables at the rear. Kid Antrim and Rusty Fergus leaned idly on the bar, smiling and lifting their glasses to Dan. They were in the early twenties, a bit younger than Dan's twenty-four years, and they regarded him as a friend and comrade rather than as the boss's son, for which Dan was duly grateful. Antrim was a slender laughing boy with a gay reckless tilt to his blond head, and Fergus was a wiry freckled redhead, as cocky as they ever come.

"Jud wants some help with the gear," Dan said. "When you boys get through drinking your breakfast."

"If you can pry Barney and the Injun loose from that pool table, Dan," drawled Kid Antrim, with a lazy graceful gesture toward the rear.

"You see Silk Coniff, Dan?" asked Rusty Fergus. "Thought I saw Haydock and Klugstad around last night, but I ain't certain."

Dan shook his head, and Antrim said laughingly: "You was drunk enough to see most anything, Redhead."

"And you was so sober I had to put you to bed, boy," said Fergus.

Dan left them arguing good-naturedly and strolled to the poolroom at the back. Barnhorst was making a run, draping his long languid frame over the table and reeling off shots with nonchalant precision. Kiowa Kempter's brawny bulk reclined on a bench by the wall, a cigar jutting from his broad coppery face, a beer mug in one huge paw.

"Call me when you're done, Barney," he growled at the ceiling. "And use the stick instead of your hands and elbows."

"You know I'm honest, Injun," said Barnhorst,

7

cutting the yellow-striped nine ball into a corner pocket and grinning at Dan.

These two were somewhat older and much larger men, the rangy Barnhorst towering inches over Dan's six-one height when he straightened up, and Kempter built wide and heavy, solid and powerful. The strong boys of Rafter, terrors in a barroom brawl once someone strained Barney's geniality and pierced the stoicism of the Indian.

"Jud Crater craves your assistance, boys," Dan Ruylander told them.

Barnhorst racked his cue. "Getting tired of massacring this Injun anyway, Dan." He strapped on his gun belt and reached for his coat.

Kempter sat up with a sigh. "Morning, Danny. Ain't that old buck got the gear to the station yet? Gave him plenty time and leeway."

"See you at the train," Dan said. "Got to meet Dad at the club."

"We'll bring them two barflies along, Dan," promised big Barney.

On the street Dan's mind reverted once more to the emigrant days his father had described so often. The traffic had started in 1842, when Tom Fitzpatrick piloted Elijah White's party of one hundred across Wyoming, the Rockies and Idaho, to the Dalles on the Columbia River in Oregon Territory. The westward movement increased with the years, its tide swollen by Brigham Young's Mormons in 1847 and the California-bound gold-seekers in 1849. The old trails—the Oregon, the Great Salt Lake and the California—were one, until they crossed South Pass and diverged west of the Continental Divide.

But the pilgrims from Pennsylvania were seeking neither a new Zion nor gold dust. They wanted land and homes in Oregon, which the Donation Land Act of 1850 promised to them free of charge. Most of them were farmers and would till the soil of the Willamette Valley. A few, like Dirk Ruylander and Owen Terrell, wanted to raise cattle out there, and Dirk was bringing the nucleus of a herd with him.

One of the most prosperous young men of the expedition, Derek Ruylander had owned his wagon and oxen, a fine Durham bull and twenty cows, a half-dozen saddle horses and a well-lined money belt. Owen Terrell, his friend, possessed nothing much but personal equipment, expense money, and a vast abundance of magnetic charm. Dirk was willing to share almost anything he had with Terrell, because he enjoyed Owen's company . . . . The one exception was a dark lovely girl named Melinda, whom Dirk Ruylander meant to marry once they were settled in Oregon. Melinda was sometimes a bit resentful of Dirk's close attachment to Owen Terrell . . . .

Now Dirk was waiting on the gallery of the Cheyenne Club, and Dan climbed the steps and a took a chair beside his father. There was a distant look in Dirk's deep gray eyes, and Dan knew he was looking back across three decades.

"It all comes back today, Dan, stronger and clearer than ever," Dirk Ruylander said. "I can see Fort Laramie as plain as the afternoon we pulled in and ringed the wagons on the river flats. Indian village outside and as many Injuns and trappers as there were soldiers around the garrison . . . . . Campfire talk of whiskey at the sutler's and willing squaws on the loose. Had a thirst after the long haul from Independence, and wanted to get inside the fort."

Melinda had ordered Dirk to stay with her, and they quarreled bitterly when he insisted on visiting the post with Owen Terrell and others from the train. This served to increase Dirk's thirst for liquor and excitement.

"Built of mud bricks with fifteen-foot walls and

palisade," Dirk went on. "Blockhouse above the entrance, clay bastions at the corners, just about as the fur traders built it in '34. Army took over in '49 but hadn't improved it much. Buildings inside were backed against the walls, with second-floor galleries over the parade and a stock compound at one end. There was whiskey at the store all right, but we didn't see any squaws. And later that poker game upstairs . . ."

Dirk Ruylander had drunk more than was his custom, and finally got into the game, which included soldiers and trappers as well as emigrants. Dan knew the story by heart, but it never failed to fascinate him. He could see the tobacco smoke clouding the hot flicker of oil lamps, a shrunken scalp on the wall, and buffalo robes strewn about the floor. Whiskey flowed like water, and Owen Terrell kept pouring more into Dirk's tin cup.

The rest was a nightmare, never clear in Dirk Ruylander's mind. The drink hit him all at once and numbed his brain. Vaguely he was aware of troopers, then traders, and finally Pennsylvania men dropping out, until it narrowed down to a two-handed affair between Dirk and Owen Terrell. And Owen was suddenly a stranger, an enemy, the evil showing through the handsome mask of his features.

Men tried to break it up, pull Dirk away from the table, but he flung them off and Owen laid his pistol on the board, warning the others to mind their own business. And Dirk had lost steadily . . . The sutler was there at the end, and then the roof fell and brought crushing blackness, as Dirk pitched headlong onto a smelly buffalo robe and passed out cold for the first time in his life . . . .

Days later Dirk Ruylander had come back to life on that same robe. Obviously he had been drugged, almost to death. For a time they thought he was going to die there.

The wagon train was long gone, and with it Dirk's

wagon and supplies, stock and equipment. As well as Melinda and Owen Terrell . . . His money belt and pockets were empty. He was cleaned out completely.

Heaving upright in red madness and reeling out to the gallery, Dirk had been bent on taking after the train and Owen Terrell, but the sutler stopped and held him there. "You ain't fit yet, man. You can't travel alone in this country nohow. Them wagons are hell-and-gone across the plains by now. Way past the North Platte and the Rattlesnakes, past Independence Rock and Split Rock and Devil's Gate. Out on the Sweetwater and heading for South Pass."

"How can I follow them?"

"Stage next month to Salt Lake City."

"Next month?" groaned Dirk, sagging weak-kneed against the rail.

"Do you no good to follow 'em anyway," the sutler said. "Look at this paper you signed. Other fella's got a copy too. You lost all you had to him, mister. Right down to the last penny."

Dirk had glanced blindly at the dirty creased sheet. His signature all right, and witnessed. He couldn't recall signing, but there it was. No legal comeback at Owen Terrell. Just have to use a gun on him.

"Tried to stop you playing," said the sutler. "Couldn't do it. Tried to keep you from signing that. You wouldn't listen to nobody. Then you went out like a snuffed candle. We thought sure you was dead."

"What am I going to do?" Dirk asked, trying to shake the sick fog from his aching head. "That sonofabitch Terrell."

"Git your health back and join the army," the sutler said. "What else can a busted man do in this godforsaken country?"

So Derek Ruylander had stayed behind to enlist in the cavalry at Fort Laramie, while Owen Terrell pushed on to Oregon and married Melinda, and started ranching in the Powder River Valley with Dirk's cattle and money. Most of the Pennsylvanians went on to settle in the Willamette, but Owen liked the looks of the country and grass along the North Powder.

Ten years later, in 1861, when gold was discovered in the John Day and Powder River Valleys of eastern Oregon, rich deposits were found on Owen Terrell's land. A wealthy man then, he had built his Triangle T into one of the largest and finest cow outfits in that country.

"When Owen struck it rich in '61, Dan," said Dirk Ruylander, "I was still a frontier trooper at fifty cents per day. Guarding stage stations, escorting emigrant trains and freight wagons, fighting the Sioux and Shoshones."

"Well, you caught up with him, Dad."

"Not quite. I always wanted to get my hands—or a gun—on him. But I never got around to it."

"You've got Rafter—and he's dead," Dan murmured. "They're both dead out there."

Dirk nodded slowly, thinking: *And with Lorna gone I'm half-dead myself, God rest her sweet soul* . . . . On furlough in Denver back in '57, Dirk had married Lorna Wade, who left a luxurious home to come to Fort Laramie and bear him two sons and a daughter. She was the reason he hadn't reached Oregon to settle the score with Owen Terrell, and she had given Dirk the incentive to leave the army and build up his own brand.

In the '60s the big war was on in the East, but out here there were still Indians to fight, and Manassas Junction and Shiloh might have been on a different planet . . . . A lieutenant by 1866 and rated one of the best field officers on the frontier, Dirk Ruylander went north with his company and scout Jud Crater to patrol and keep open the Bozeman Road, which led to the gold fields and mines of Montana.

After the Fetterman Massacre in December of '66, the

12

northern garrisons were withdrawn. Dirk resigned his commission, left his family at the Wade mansion in Denver, and rode into the Southwest with Jud Crater, comrade of many campaigns. For a season they hunted buffalo, and saved their money instead of blowing it.

Then they got riding jobs down there and helped trail-drive some of the first big herds from Texas to Wyoming. Thereafter Dirk's rise had been rapid, as he worked his way up from cowboy to tophand to ramrod, and then branched out to establish Rafter R and make it one of the finest ranches in the Sweetwater country, with tough little Jud Crater as his foreman. Wyoming cattle business boomed in the 1870s, and Dirk Ruylander was riding the crest of the wave.

He never forgot or forgave Owen Terrell and Melinda, but he was too busy raising his family and building up Rafter to make the long trek to Oregon . . . Now in 1881, thirty years after that poker game in old Fort Laramie, Dirk Ruylander wanted some shorthorn stock from Oregon to round out his herds. After scouting out there the previous year, Jud Crater had reported both Owen and Melinda Terrell dead, with Triangle being operated by their son Garry and their daughter Sue . . . .

"You don't think too much of this deal, do you, Dan?" asked Dirk.

"I didn't say that, Dad," protested Dan, with discomfort.

Dirk smiled and clapped him on the shoulder. "Let's go in and have a drink or two for the road, son. I've been talking—and thinking—too goddamn much here. And it's getting on toward train time."

They rose together, tall and straight and easy, and Dan said earnestly: "Don't think I don't want to go, Dad."

Dirk pressed his arm with warm affection and pride. "I'm not worried about you, Danny. I wouldn't be

13

sending you out there if I didn't believe you were right and ready, and big enough for the job."

Two

Dirk Ruylander eased off the gleaming bar, one of Brunswicke-Balke-Callander's most elaborate products, and examined his gold watch. "Time to go, son. Heard her whistle down the line." He raised his glass in a great gnarled hand. "To you and your trip, Dan. Out and back."

Dan smiled and drank with him, and they walked out through the blue haze of expensive cigars and the plush furnishings of the Cheyenne Club, two big men marked with a strong family resemblance. Other members called or waved to Dirk, some wanting to talk with him, but he couldn't spare the time at present. Dan wondered if he'd ever be as well-liked and respected as his father. It was doubtful. Few men had the natural sincerity and charm, the easy friendliness and warm human quality of Derek Ruylander.

Descending the broad staircase from the high porch, they walked toward the railroad station in windtorn sunshine and dust. Dan glanced back once at the cupola and heavy mansard roof of the clubhouse, its exterior ugliness belying the inner comfort and elegance. He never felt quite at home there. He was just old Dirk Ruylander's boy, and it hurt something in his shy sensitive nature to be dismissed that way. The sons of big men were never supposed to amount to much, but Dan thought he might be an exception. Well, this mission to the far west ought to determine whether he was or not.

"Always wanted to take this trip myself, Dan," mused Dirk, as they matched long strides on the crusty worn planks of the sidewalk. "Figured on it for thirty years but never got around to going. Now I'm too old, I reckon. Owen Terrell and his wife both dead out there, and there isn't much point in my going to Oregon."

They paused on the station platform, and Dirk chewed his cigar and studied his son. It was like seeing himself in a mirror thirty-odd years back, only Dan was a trifle taller and slimmer, and maybe better looking. But Dan had the same tawny hair and gray eyes, the proud nose and wide pleasant mouth, the firm chin and strong jawbones of the Ruylanders. That winning smile and easy assurance of movement and manner. My boy all right, thought Dirk. I couldn't have done better with Melinda. Probably not near as good. Lorna was more woman than the other, a real thoroughbred. Lorna was the right one for me, and I'm sure glad I got ditched here in Wyoming.

"Don't be taken in by young Garry Terrell—or the girl either," Dirk said. "They're apt to be as smooth and likable as their dad was, and no more to be trusted. I haven't been fooled by too many men, Dan, but Owen Terrell did a good job of it."

Dan Ruylander was silent, feeling suddenly young and callow and inadequate, already lonesome and homesick in this moment of parting. Uncomfortably conscious of the wealth in his money belt, the weight of responsibility and command on his shoulders. The locomotive whistle floated in with a mournful sound, and people around the depot began to stir and gather luggage.

"Rode all the cattle trails, but never the west end of the Oregon that I started out on," Dirk said, made voluble by unaccustomed emotion. "Well, that's the way it goes, and it don't matter much now. I've got you to send, Danny, and I wouldn't ask for a better man."

15

Dan felt vaguely embarrassed, unworthy and immature and uncertain. He wondered if his father really meant that, or was just trying to bolster up his son's courage. Dan had proved himself pretty well on the home range and in drives up from the Southwest, but this was another matter. He was on his own, in charge for the first time, on a mission that loomed ever larger and harder. All the way to Baker City, Oregon, to trail-drive three thousand head of shorthorns back to Wyoming. With complications far beyond those of normal business transactions and hardships of the trail.

"Five good men with you, Dan," said Dirk, as if sensing his apprehension. "Jud's been out there and knows the country. He'll help you plenty—but remember you're the boss on this one. Kempter's solid and so's big Barney. The young fellas, Antrim and Fergus, are kinda wild and chancy but good boys. But you know all this, Danny . . . . Pick careful when it comes to picking six riders out there. And when it comes to standing up to the goddamn Terrells don't feel any pity for 'em. You know the story, son."

Yes, Dan knew it all right. He had grown up with it. From boyhood on, he had been nurtured in hatred for the Terrells, shaped and tempered subtly into a living instrument of revenge. Now, at twenty-four, the time had come to strike. His father was hurling him across the western third of the continent like a human spear, driven at the heart of the Terrells and their Triangle ranch.

The train pulled in and shuddered to a halt, with a few passengers getting off and many more climbing aboard. Mormons on their way to settle in Utah, and prospectors headed for the mining camps of Idaho.

"Maybe foolish to hold a grudge for thirty years, Dan," murmured Dirk. "I don't feel it like I used to, but I'd still like to collect a little something from the Terrells."

Jud Crater and the other Rafter hands boarded the train, burdened with saddles and warbags, and Dan knew they were taking care of his gear as well as their own. He looked at Dirk and saw how age and toil had bowed and shriveled his father, gaunting the fine features and silvering the sandy hair. Dirk had aged since Mom's death.

"You take care of yourself, Dad, and the kids," Dan said, with a sudden terrible loneliness and longing for his dead mother gripping him like a chill.

Dirk snorted softly. "I'll be all right, boy. The kids'll take care of me. Judy keeps the house almost as good as your mother did, and Hudson's a better business man already than I ever was." He spoke with quiet pride of Dan's younger sister and brother. "I got a lot to be thankful for, Danny, lucky in all my children. Two kids like them, and a man like you to finish the trip I started on thirty years ago. You know, Dan, some of those Durhams you drive back will be descended from the stock I started west in '51."

"I thought of that, Dad," said Dan. "Well, I better be getting on."

They shook hands firmly, and Dirk said: "Thought I saw Coniff and Haydock and Klugstad taking the train. If they're on, watch out for 'em, Danny. They're poison-mean sonsabitches."

"I will, Dad." He turned away, hollow and desolate, trying to blink the sting from his eyeballs. From the coach steps Dan glanced back at his father, but Dirk was busily engaged in relighting his cigar . . . . The engine was getting up steam, the wide stack belching black smoke and fiery sparks and coarse cinders. With bell clanging the train jerked into motion, jolting and lurching, and the long journey westward was started.

Swaying along the car in search of his companions, Dan Ruylander saw the three men his father had mentioned. Bull Klugstad and Tip Haydock were seated

17

with their backs toward Dan, facing forward. He recognized the thick red neck and massive shoulders of Klugstad, and the beak-nosed profile of Haydock. Lounging on the arm of the next seat, striped trousers and silver-inlaid boots in the aisle, was Silk Coniff. Thumbs in gun belt, the insolent curve of his lips reflected in his cold brilliant eyes, Coniff was baiting the two young men across the aisle. Easterners in cheap store suits, pale from sickness or from inside living, trying to ignore Coniff and conceal their fright.

"If you're Mormons where are your women?" demanded Coniff. "You mean to say you haven't got a bunch of wives yet? What the hell kind of Mormons are you anyway? Probably you figure the Saints'll furnish you with wives in Salt Lake City. Quite a breeding pen they got out there. Whores and whoremasters."

His victims sat stiff and speechless with eyes front, waiting miserably for Coniff to tire of this sport. Dan wondered what these three hardcase characters were traveling west for. No good, that was for sure. They made a living stealing stock from Rafter and the other big spreads, along with their crooked gambling. Holdups in this country were generally accredited to Silk Coniff's outfit, but they never got caught at it. Some thought they worked with Cattle Kate Maxwell and Jim Averill.

"Mormons are supposed to be great studs," Coniff continued relentlessly. "But you boys don't look as if you could serve any brood of women. Maybe they geld the weaklings like you though. Strange things go on in that Tabernacle in New Jerusalem, they say."

Dan Ruylander stepped forward and said quietly: "Cut it out, Silk."

Coniff turned with his quick scornful smile. "Why howdy, friend Dan. Didn't know you were on board. Maybe you'll set into a little game of cards here."

"No, thanks. Where you boys going, Silk?"

18

"Has Rafter taken over the U.P.? I didn't know you were running the railroad too, Dan. I could ask where you're going, but I'm too much of a gentleman."

"You don't know?" Dan murmured, with mild disbelief. "You didn't know where Ben Campbell was going last year either, did you?"

Silk Coniff came erect off the chair-arm, still smiling but with a new menace in it. "That's a nasty insinuation, Dan. You looking for trouble?" Klugstad was watching with a baleful red-eyed glare, while Haydock looked on with icy indifference.

"No place for trouble, Silk," said Dan Ruylander. "Just leave those two boys alone."

"I'm taking orders from you? I don't think so, Danny. You aren't *that* big."

"Don't push too hard, Silk."

Coniff laughed lightly. "You're the one that's on the prod, boy. But we've got nothing to fight about. No secret where we're going, Dan. Got a little business in Utah."

"Business?" Dan said, with irony.

"We ain't big business like Rafter," Coniff said, in mock humility. "But we get along all right in a small way."

"You sure do," agreed Dan Ruylander.

The restrained hatred was there between them, as it had been from the first. They had fought once when Coniff presumed to dance with Dan's sister Judith, a bloody savage brawl that ended about even . . . . Sometime they'd face one another over the gun barrels, and it would be to the death. They both knew it, and secretly dreaded the inevitable showdown. The shadow of it was always hanging over their heads.

Dan moved on past Coniff, and Silk spoke contemptuously behind him: "Now listen to this, you Mormon scum, and don't be thinking that I've been scared off of you. I'm—"

19

He broke off and reached for his holster, as Dan wheeled back in flaring anger and lashed out with his left hand. It caught Coniff under the jawbone with a solid smash, twisting his head and driving him backward. Haydock and Klugstad had started to rise and draw, but Coniff sprawled heavily across them, pinning them down in the seat.

Floundering and thrashing around, Silk Coniff came upright and lunged at Ruylander in the aisle. Dan hit him with a right this time, that ripped through Silk's flailing arms and snapped his neck almost to the breaking point. Once more Coniff landed on top of his struggling partners. They heaved up and flung him off into the opposite seat, grabbing for their guns then, but Dan Ruylander's Colt was already clear and lined on them. Klugstad and Haydock sank back on the sooty cushions, and Coniff lay stunned and bleeding in front of them.

Dan motioned to the Mormons. "Why don't you boys try the next car? The air's better up there." They got up hastily and moved forward with relief.

"You ain't seen the last of us, Danny boy," grated Bull Klugstad.

"I hope not. It'd be awful lonesome without you three," Ruylander said gravely. "Tell Silk I'll use a gun on him next time."

"Don't scare us so, son," drawled Tip Haydock, a grimace on his bony big-nosed face.

The conductor came rushing down the aisle, and Dan sheathed his gun as the man asked: "What's going on here? Oh, it's you, Dan. What's the matter anyway?"

"Those three belong in a cattle car," Dan Ruylander said. "But if you haven't got one, I suppose people will have to put up with them."

"You want 'em thrown off in Laramie, Dan?"

"Not unless they start more trouble. They've got a big business deal in Utah."

The conductor snorted. "God help the poor Mormons. I'll keep an eye on them, Dan. Your crew's up ahead in the next car."

Dan Ruylander walked along the lurching train, accepted the thanks of the two young Mormons, and dropped into the seat Jud Crater had saved for him. Across the aisle Kid Antrim was sitting with Rusty Fergus, while Barnhorst and Kiowa Kempter shared the seat facing them. Dan reported the presence of the Coniff trio in the coach behind them.

"I saw 'em in Cheyenne," said Jud Crater, eyes slitted and mouth bitter in his scarred leathery face. "Thought maybe they'd tag along."

"Probably going to hold up the train," Kid Antrim remarked, laughing and tossing his fair head. "That's all the bastards are good for."

"More likely aiming to jump us," Kiowa Kempter growled, his stern Indian features darkly impassive. "I hope the sonsabitches do."

"Like they did Ben Campbell," said big Barnhorst, mentioning the Anvil trail boss who had been murdered and robbed on his way to buy a herd in Baker City. "They ain't paid for that yet, goddamn 'em."

"Ben was alone," Rusty Fergus reminded, scratching his red hair. "They ain't going to come at six of us. I wish they would, but they sure as hell won't. They want the odds running their way."

"They could figure on us getting split up somewhere along," old Jud Crater rasped, shifting his chew from one seamed cheek to the other. "Or on catching Dan alone sometime. They know we're going out to buy cattle, and they want that sixty thousand they expect we're toting. So we'd better hang pretty close together, boys."

"It's time somebody blasted that christly Coniff crew," said Kid Antrim, his boyish face hard and smooth. "Taken too much a their cheap horseshit."

Jud Crater nodded. "True enough, Kid. But it's tough to beat a stacked deck or bullets in the back. Which is the only way them three like to throw their lead."

Dan Ruylander was sober and thoughtful. The appearance of Silk Coniff and his two lieutenants bothered Dan more than he would have cared to admit. He had enough on his mind without worrying about those badmen from the home Territory.

Three

About forty miles west of Cheyenne at Tie Siding, the railroad made an abrupt bend northward for its run into Laramie. "These towns sprung up when the Union Pacific started building across Wyoming in '67," Jud Crater mused beside Dan Ruylander. "About the time your dad and me cut loose from the army and hit for the southwest cattle country. Dirk was planning on a brand of his own way back then. He always claimed the bunch and buffalo grass on these plains would fatten stock in the summer and stay good through the winter. But when the first legislature of this Territory gave women the vote in '69, Dirk and me damn near decided to stay down Texas way."

Dan listened drowsily, lulled by the rocking motion, the click of iron wheels over steel rail-joints, and the blurred somnolent sound that voices have on a train. Outside the murky cinder-flecked windows, the spring sunlight shimmered brightly on sagebrush flats and rolling grasslands, broken by reddish erosion buttes and mesas and gaunt hogback ridges. Tree growth was restricted mainly to the waterways, the hills and mountains.

Thirty years back the emigrants had plodded along the westward trail with ox-drawn wagons, their course roughly parallel to and some sixty miles north of the present railroad line. Now in 1881 you could ride the U.P. as far as Ogden, Utah, and take the Holladay Stage Line from there to Baker City, Oregon. Traveling expenses were about $75 per man, Dirk Ruylander had estimated, but railway freight rates were still high enough to prohibit shipment of cattle. With a good trail boss, an experienced crew, and luck, a herd could be driven from Oregon to Wyoming for approximately a dollar a head.

Dan had all these and many other figures in his head—and so much money on him it scared him to think of it. Over $60,000 . . . . He envied the other Rafter riders, who were feeling free and rich and independent, with the five $20 gold pieces Dirk had handed each of them resting agreeably in their pockets.

In 1876, a treaty with the Sioux and Cheyennes at the Red Cloud Agency in Nebraska, had opened up new graze on the rich plains of Wyoming. Texas cattle were now going to the railhead at Dodge City, the last and longest-lived of the Kansas trail towns, and thence directly to Eastern markets. A new source of beef was needed by the Wyoming ranchers.

The movement of Idaho and Oregon stock into Wyoming had begun in 1879, when the first Carter Company herds were driven from the vicinity of Fort Bridger to the South Fork of the Stinking Water, in Big Horn Basin. More and more Wyoming stockmen were building up their herds in this fashion, oblivious to warnings against overstocking the range, and Dirk Ruylander had decided it was an ideal time to make his long-delayed move against the Terrells . . . "Three thousand head won't settle the account," Dirk said. "Forty-five thousand dollars worth of beef isn't near enough. But it'll help some, Danny."

From Laramie the train labored on in a northwesterly direction, with the Medicine Bow Range humped to the left and the Laramie Mountains piled on the right. Across the Laramie River at Bosler, and on through Lookout and Rock River to the town of Medicine Bow, where the railroad started its long and relatively straight drive westward over sweeping barren plains that looked endless as an ocean, amber, green and dun, silvered with sage under the sun.

Nearing the supper-stop in Rawlins, about two hundred miles out of Cheyenne, the afternoon was on the wane with the sun sinking redly beyond western ramparts. It was a relief to get away from the sooty stench of the train and stretch their legs, belly up to a bar for a couple of drinks and then eat a quick meal. Dan Ruylander and his comrades were on the watch for the Coniff threesome, but did not spot them. Rafter lay about seventy miles northwest of here, and Rawlins was the station generally used by rail travelers from the home ranch.

Back in the coach they settled down again for the all-night ride across the western stretches of Wyoming, the Red Desert virtually uninhabited for some eighty miles west of Rawlins. A bleak wasteland until they reached the tributaries of the Green River around Rock Springs.

"Get some sleep, Dan," advised Jud Crater. "Man my age don't need much."

On the other side of the aisle young Antrim and Fergus were already sleeping like children, and the stolid Kempter was snoring softly beside Barnhorst's towering bulk. Dan tried to relax, stop thinking and submerge himself in slumber, but he only dozed in fitful snatches. His brain kept working and whirling, his thoughts spinning and tumbling about like dice in a chuckaluck cage, and the cindery foulness of the train pervaded everything.

He wondered what Garry and Sue Terrell were like, and if he could sustain hatred against them as he had against their parents, for what they had done to his dad. He strove to visualize how things would have turned out, if Dirk Ruylander had gone on to Oregon and married Melinda. Would Dan and his brother and sister exist now, or would the offspring be Garry and Sue? Or someone entirely different from any of them? It was beyond Dan. He remembered the picture of Melinda in the gold locket his father had; the only thing Owen Terrell left on him in the sutler's loft at Fort Laramie, either by accident or design. Lovelier but less nice than Dan's mother . . . Would Sue look like that? Would something in Dan's blood and flesh make him fall in love with Sue, instead of hating her?

Garry Terrell had the reputation of being good with a gun, Jud Crater told them, but that didn't trouble Dan too much. From Dirk and Jud he had learned to handle guns, as he had learned to ride and rope, work stock, read brands and signs, and trail-drive a herd. Dan was educated and conditioned for life on the range, and he doubted if there were any better teachers than his dad and Jud in the whole West. So he was ready on that score, if he had to fight Garry Terrell with fists or six guns or Winchesters. But the girl Sue was a different proposition. You couldn't beat or shoot a woman.

Then there was the Coniff crew to consider. Silk had always wanted to destroy Dan, and now the fortune in Dan's money belt gave him all the more incentive. Somewhere along the way west Coniff would make his try, and since the odds favored Rafter it was apt to come from ambush or behind Dan's back. Just another complication, a constant nagging irritant.

Resentment grew in Dan Ruylander as he twisted his cramped body on the hard cushions. Sometimes this whole venture seemed pointless and meaningless to him, as much as he loved and admired his father. Owen and

Melinda Terrell were dead and buried, and that should have closed the chapter and ended the feud. You cannot hate the dead, and you should not hate their descendants. Dirk Ruylander didn't really need the Oregon cattle or the profit from this deal. Dirk had rebounded from a disastrous start in Wyoming Territory to make a good life and marriage and a great success of Rafter, even though it had come much slower and harder than for Owen Terrell, since Dirk had started empty-handed from scratch. Now Dirk had outlived those other two, and he should have dropped the matter when he heard they were dead and gone.

Anger at himself touched Dan then, as the miles clanked away in the moonlit night. What the hell are you crying for, boy? he thought disgustedly. Is your first big job so tough it's got you hunting a gopher hole to crawl into? Is this too much to do for a father that's given you everything all your life? Buck up and be a man, for godsake. The kind of man that old Dirk Ruylander deserves for a son. Ride it out, cowboy. You're twenty-four and full-grown, and this is your first chance to pay back a little of what you owe your old man. You'd better measure up to it.

Stations and stops were more frequent toward morning, and the Aspen Mountains loomed like a ghost range in the southern grayness. They caught a quick breakfast in Green River, and the train rattled on over the stream that had given its name to that settlement.

"The Mormons came down this way from South Pass," said Jud Crater. "Thousands after thousands of 'em, some walking and pushing handcarts all the way from Missouri. And folks today think it's rough riding the rails. People have grown christawful soft."

It was still about a hundred miles to the Utah border, with a lot of whistle stops along the line, and the coach became stifling hot again as the sun soared higher behind the train. Fretted by close confinement and vile odors, the Rafter men took turns walking up and down the cars. Dan Ruylander had his stroll with Kid Antrim and Rusty Fergus, and observed that the Coniff party was no longer in the coach behind theirs.

"Probably riding in style in the Pullman," laughed Antrim. "On money from the Rafter beef they been rustling." In this country sleepers were considered suitable for womenfolk and drummers, invalids and the aged. Punchers preferred drinking in the day coaches.

"Maybe they got off somewhere," Fergus suggested.

"I don't think so, Rusty," said Dan. "We're going to have them on our backs all the way to Baker City."

"Unless we blow 'em off and burn 'em down," Kid Antrim said, hitching the gun belt on his trim hips. "Which would pleasure me a lot."

Back in his seat at Jud Crater's side, Dan stared out the dirty window at the Uinta Mountains which rose in rugged splendor to the south, running parallel to the railroad and dominated by King Peak, as Jud pointed out.

"It sure is educational to travel with Old Man Crater," grinned Kid Antrim.

Jud grunted and big Barnhorst said: "You can stand educating, Kid, if anybody ever could."

"Look who's talking!" jeered Antrim. "The biggest and dumbest guy east of the Rockies."

Around noontime there was a brief halt for dinner in Evanston, on the Bear River. There was still no sign of Coniff and Haydock and Klugstad in the depot restaurant. Soon afterward the train chugged across the border into Utah, and Dan saw the mighty Wasatch Range, rearing in stark jagged grandeur and stretching far southward down the center of the territory.

"They tell me this Valley Tan they got here is real good drinking liquor," remarked Rusty Fergus. "And I sure got an awful dry."

"It's a mite strong for younkers like you and the Kid,

Redhead," laughed Barnhorst.

"Right, Barney," agreed Kiowa Kempter. "Couple rounds and they'll be flat in the sawdust."

"Well, we can rest our feet on 'em under the table, Injun," said Barnhorst.

Jud Crater munched sourly on his tobacco. "We'll hit Ogden sometime this afternoon. Late probably, at the rate this thing goes. But there ain't going to be no big drinking bout, boys."

"Why not, Jud?" asked Kid Antrim. "All we got to do tomorrow is ride a stage coach. Even Barney can stay on a rig like that."

"Reckon we'll run across Silk Coniff and his pardners tonight in Ogden," said Jud Crater. "Maybe that's one good reason for staying fairly sober."

"Jud's right, boys," Dan Ruylander said seriously. "We'll have to take it kind of easy."

Antrim and Fergus eyed him with mild surprise and consternation. Dan was usually the ringleader when Rafter set out to hurrah and tree some frontier town. Some hellhole like Rongis, back in Wyoming.

Four

Ogden, Utah, was a busy place when the train arrived in the late afternoon. The streets were clogged with huge freight wagons. The boardwalks swarmed with miners, emigrants and townsmen, ranchers, cowboys and farmers, drifters and gamblers and blanket Indians. The signs of numerous saloons and gambling halls showed above the overhangs jutting from high false-fronted structures, as the train jarred to a grinding stop.

The Rafter crew gathered up warbags and carbines,

saddles and gear, and climbed down the car steps with relief, inhaling the open air and stretching their stiffened limbs. They loitered on the crowded platform until they saw Silk Coniff and his two companions emerge from the rear coach and vanish into the thronged street. The vultures were still with them all right. Then Jud Crater led them across the way to the stage station, where they deposited their belongings and arranged for passage on a northbound stage in the morning.

"Boy, oh man, look at all them goddamn barrooms and honkytonks!" Kid Antrim said, as they came out and stood under the depot awning to roll cigarettes and survey the seething main drag. After the long chafing railroad journey the boys were raring to go, and Dan Ruylander did not blame them in the least. Under different circumstances he would have been more than ready to cut loose with them himself.

They washed up at a backyard pump and trough, had a few drinks in the nearest saloon, and then supper in the foremost hotel. There were no rooms available, as Crater had anticipated, but he said they would take their bedrolls and sleep in the stage company barn.

"Be a lot more comfortable in a nice cosy parlor house," Rusty Fergus said, grinning and winking at Antrim. "Ain't had any for a spell."

"Sure, you want to spend that hundred before you get anywhere near Oregon," laughed Barnhorst. "And not get any sleep besides."

In the evening, with the freighters still rumbling northward for the Snake River Valley, the gold fields of the Beaverhead country and other Idaho mining camps, they wandered about town in a tight group and smoked after-supper cigars, eyes alert under hatbrims and guns loosened in the leather. Until Rusty Fergus and Kid Antrim went astray after some dance-hall pretties, while Kiowa Kempter and big Barnhorst succumbed to the

29

lure of the gaming tables in the Royal Casino.

Jud Crater didn't like this, and Dan Ruylander was somewhat perturbed. But you couldn't keep strict military discipline in a cow outfit. Particularly after the boys had been imprisoned on the Iron Horse of the Union Pacific. And those four punchers could take care of themselves, even in the cathouses and gambling joints.

In a place called the Gold Nugget, Jud and Dan sat at an out-of-the-way table and nursed their drinks in a slow thoughtful manner.

"You like the idea of this trip, son?" inquired Crater.

"Not altogether, Jud."

"Me neither, Dan. But Dirk was set on it. Couldn't talk him out of it. Your mother might've, but nobody else could . . . . Well, you'll see some country and maybe learn quite a bit."

"What are the Terrells like?" asked Dan, squinting his gray eyes against the smoke.

Jud Crater spat at a brass cuspidor. "Right nice to meet. I didn't get to know 'em well enough to really tell. The boy's big and good-looking, about your size. Well thought of out there. Got a tough gun-hung crew working for Triangle. One real bad sonofabitch by the name of Hawk Fallon."

"Is the girl pretty, Jud?"

"No beauty but she's got something. Kind of a thoroughbred look. Clear features and clean lines, a way of talking and moving. Men would go for her, even if she wasn't half-owner of the biggest layout on the Powder. You'll maybe fall yourself, son."

Dan smiled solemnly. "That would seem almost like incest, Jud."

Aware of someone staring fixedly at him, Dan Ruylander glanced around until he reached a group of percentage girls. The coppery-haired one in the green dress had her eye on him. She smiled with bright warmth, looking younger and fresher than most of the women, and Dan felt a little flattered, even though he knew how mercenary these calico queens were . . . . In a few minutes she walked toward their table with easy grace, slender yet full-bodied in the tight green satin, and Dan saw that she had green eyes with that auburn hair.

"Buy a girl a drink?"

"No," Jud Crater said, with flat distate.

"Come on, Jud. We can afford one," Dan said casually.

The girl sat down close to Dan, her knee and thigh touching his beneath the table, and he ordered another round. "My name's Sadie," she said. "Is he your father? Or your grampaw?"

"His godfather," said Jud. "And I say to hell with you."

Sadie laughed softly. "Some old-timers get that way, after they've had their fling. But I'll bet *he* isn't over the hill yet. It's all right, Pop. I just want to talk to your godson. I haven't seen anything else since he came in." She turned to Dan. "What's your name?"

"Dan Ruylander."

"A fine name. It fits you, too. Are you going to Idaho? I've got to get up there myself—sometime."

The drinks came, and even Jud Crater raised his glass to Sadie. The girl had a certain charm, a clean wholesome quality for one in this trade. The frank interest in her green eyes and the warm pressure of her leg stirred Dan deeply. Women were scarce in the cattle country, and it was some time since Dan had been with a girl. A long time since he'd been near one as appealing as Sadie. He wished he was alone with her now, and old Jud was sound asleep in the Holladay barn.

"You up from Texas, Dan?" she asked. When he told her Wyoming, she said: "Hard to tell the difference. But I knew you weren't from out here. I came from Oregon, and I'm thinking of going back there. Good old Baker City on the Powder.''

"Baker City?"

"Sure, what's wrong with that? You know Baker City? Or maybe you're heading that way? If you are take me with you. Please, I won't be any trouble. And I can pay my own way.''

"Can't do that, Sadie," said Dan.

"You can take the stage anytime, gal," Jud Cratr said, his narrow bleached eyes scanning her sharply, his wizened brown face ironic. "Who set you onto us tonight? A bastard named Coniff maybe?''

Sadie shook her head, the red-gold highlights glimmering in her hair. "I don't know any Coniff. Dan, won't you come with me? Where we can talk in private. You're of age, aren't you?"

Dan wanted to go with her. His blood was racing from the firm silken fullness of her thigh against his. He wanted her with a hard rising urgency, but he could not leave old Jud.

"Sorry, Sadie," he murmured. "Might be trouble tonight. We've got to stick together."

"So you're gunfighters?"

"No, we're just cattle men," Dan said. "But there are some gunnies on our trail."

Jud Crater made the spittoon ring with a vicious spurt of tobacco juice. "Tell her everything you know, Dan," he grumbled, in disgust. "Let's get out of this cheap trap. She ain't interested in your life story. She's interested in the money in your pocket, boy.''

"You aren't the smartest old man in the world, Pop," said Sadie, her green eyes alight. "Take all the money Dan's got on him, and he can still come with me. It won't cost him a copper, Pop. I'll even pay for the drinks.''

Jud Crater grinned bleakly at her. "Because somebody's paying you to take him out of circulation for a spell. I've seen your kind from here to the Rio Grande.''

The girl gestured hopelessly. "You've got me all wrong, for some reason. But I guess there's no use in arguing . . . I wanted Dan for himself. It hit me when he walked in that door. Like a flash of lightning.''

"How often you get hit that way, gal?" Jud asked coldly.

"Not so often as you think, Pop. Not once since I left Baker City—about three years ago. But why waste my breath on you? You win, Pop. Take him away." Sadie rose and strode swiftly across the room.

Dan Ruylander watched her go with regret and yearning. "You were pretty rough on the girl, Jud,'' he said slowly.

"Had to be, Danny, to get rid of her. Just another goddamn floozie.''

"You could be wrong about her.''

"It's possible. But it ain't very likely, son.''

Dan smiled at him. "From what I hear, Jud, you weren't any angel at my age.''

"That's the truth,'' Jud Crater confessed gravely. "I was a ring-tailed heller from way back. A kid in my teens I made some of them rendezvous the old mountain men held in South Pass, and I wrastled with many a young Injun squaw during them crazy drunken jamborees. And that was only the beginning, Dan . . . But I wasn't out on a big job for my old man, with three killers on my tail bent on stealing my old man's money.''

"You're right, Jud,'' said Dan Ruylander gently. "You're always right. I ought to know it by now.''

Jud Crater wagged his lean gray head. "I ain't always right, Danny. Maybe most of the time but not always. I could be dead wrong about that gal, Sadie. But even so this ain't the time to get tangled up with her . . . . I'm owing you a night's fun, I reckon. I'll pay off when we

33

get that herd back to the Sweetwater next fall, Dan, and hit Front Street in Laramie. Or John Signor's in Rongis."

"You don't owe me anything, Jud," said Dan. "I'm probably in debt to you instead tonight . . . I'm glad now that she's gone. But she was kinda sweet, at that."

"She was plenty cute and sweet, son," agreed Jud Crater. "And I don't blame you a damn bit for craving some of that. But it don't really matter much one way or another, unless a man's deep in love."

Sadie was hastening back toward their table, when bedlam broke loose in the street outside. The old familiar warcry, "Rafter! Hey, Rafter!" sounded through the general uproar. Dan and Jud were already up and on their way, leaving Sadie standing there with an anguished expression straining her pert features. Dan Ruylander shouldered and elbowed men aside, with bowlegged little Jud Crater in his turbulent wake. They slammed out through the swing-doors, and saw men spewed out of the Red Lantern dance hall in a brawling torrent. A hitch-rack gave with a splintering crash, spilling embattled humanity into the street, with horses rearing and pitching about the boiling mass. Dust billowed in yellow lamplight, and the hoarse panting shout came again: "Rafter here! Hey, *Rafter!*"

On the run Dan and Jud bucked and sliced their way through milling ranks toward the scene of action. Kid Antrim and Rusty Fergus, still on their feet in midstreet, were back-to-back in the center of a savage wolf-pack, slashing away with both hands to fight off the gang that surrounded them. Dan glimpsed the Kid's blond head bobbing beside the fiery thatch of Rusty. They were making a magnificent stand against heavy odds, but Antrim and Fergus went under before Dan and Jud could break in there, overwhelmed and beaten down by sheer weight of numbers.

Big Barnhorst and Kiowa Kempter had burst out of

the nearby Royal and plunged to the rescue of their mates, tearing into that thrashing tangle and flinging bodies right and left with their terrible hands and tremendous power. Barney and the Indian were at their best in this kind of combat, Barney towering and long-armed, Kiowa broad and solid as a great rock. With amazing and destructive force and speed, they cleared a ragged gaping path to the middle of the melee, and began hauling men off Antrim and Fergus and heaving them bodily into the surging circle of spectators. The crowd gasped in astonishment as Barnhorst and Kempter smashed opponents to earth or sent them flying through the dusty night air.

Dan Ruylander was about to drive in after them, when Jud Crater restrained him with a firm hand and a crisp-voiced, "Look there, Danny. Them three bastards we got to watch."

On the opposite side Coniff and Klugstad and Haydock hovered intently on the inner rim of onlookers, hands on gun butts, watching and waiting for a clear shot at the embroiled Rafter riders. Dan drew his gun, and old Jud's Colt was already out. They started edging around the ring toward the three gunmen, the ranks yielding before their drawn pistols.

An aisle opened abruptly between the two factions, and Silk Coniff spotted them, nudging the men on either side of him. Silk trembled on the verge of drawing, but thought better of it as Dan and Jud thumbed back their hammers. Silk let go of his gun and made an open-palmed gesture of submission. Bull Klugstad dropped his right hand in spread-fingered disgust, his brute-face sullen and malevolent. But the lanky Tip Haydock took a chance, heedless of the massed mob in the street, and threw his gun clear and blazing. The slug seared between Dan and Jud, close enough to tug hotly at their coat sleeves, and someone uttered a groaning curse in the background.

Before Dan and Jud could fire back, the crowd closed in and the three outlaws were gone, scrambling and scattering through the packed assemblage. Silk Coniff headed for the alley beyond the Royal Casino, while Tip Haydock and Bull Klugstad disappeared in other directions.

The rough-and-tumble ruckus was over by this time, the odds more than evened by big Barney and Kiowa Kempter. Kid Antrim and Rusty Fergus were back on their feet, bloody, tattered and dirt-smeared, but grinning cheerfully through the sweat and grime. Their assailants had fled, except for four who lay sprawled senseless in the gravel and a couple more who were crawling blindly on hands and knees. The man hit by Haydock's shot was merely grazed on the arm.

Noting this and still holding his gun, Dan Ruylander broke away from Jud Crater and took after Silk Coniff, leaving Jud to cover the audience and rejoin the rest of the Rafter hands.

At the alley mouth gunflame speared toward Dan from the inner blackness, and he blasted back at the muzzle flash and heard his bullet rip splinters from the rear corner. Then Coniff was running again, and Dan raced through the passage to pick up his trace in the back lots. From the sounds Silk was doubling back toward the center of Ogden, and Dan stalked after him through a dark reeking labyrinth of refuse barrels, garbage dumps, ash heaps and sheds. Tin cans and bottles rolled underfoot, and clothes lines were strung in places.

Silk Coniff's boots set up a tinny jangle ahead, and Dan Ruylander fired swiftly at the sound, drawing a return shot that whipped warmly past his left shoulder. Silk crossed a thin shaft of lamplight from some window, and vanished into the backyard of another building. When Dan reached that corner a door opened, silhouetting the immaculate back of Silk Coniff and the coppery head of a woman inside. Dan held his fire, not wanting to hit the girl, even though she deserved it . . . . Silk stepped inside and the door closed instantly.

It was the rear end of the Gold Nugget, and the girl named Sadie had admitted Silk Coniff. So old Jud had been one hundred per cent correct about her . . . With a bitter taste in his mouth, not entirely from the gunpowder, Dan Ruylander punched out the empties, thumbed fresh .44 shells into the cylinder, and cut back toward the street. It would be suicide to go into a joint like the Nugget after a badman like Silk Coniff. The bastard had got away one more time.

In the street Jud Crater was still bawling out Antrim and Fergus, while Barnhorst and Kempter tried to pry some information out of their battered and half-conscious victims.

"I still say you ought to know better than start a frigging ball like that," Jud declared, spitting with explosive emphasis. "Ain't you goddamn kids ever going to grow up?"

"I tell you we never started it, Jud," protested Kid Antrim, wiping the blood off his lips and chin with his neckerchief.

"That's right, Jud," panted Rusty Fergus, rubbing his welted jawbone indignantly. "Honest to God, man. They just climbed all over us with no warning whatsoever, the horseshit sonsabitches."

"Yeah, I know it, boys," Jud Crater said, relenting at last. "Coniff set 'em on you, I reckon. He and his sidekicks was standing by looking for a chance to get a few slugs into you." He turned deliberately to Dan. "And you, you got less brains than these two pups, Danny. Hightailing it off into the back alleys with that money belt on you. What in hell was you thinking of, boy?"

"I wanted to get Silk Coniff off our necks for good, Jud," said Dan Ruylander mildly. "But I couldn't catch

37

him . . . . We'll hang together the rest of the evening, boys. Least we can do is get to Oregon without getting shot up."

"In fact, we'll all bed down right now," Jud Crater said. "That stage ride's going to be bad enough without any of you being rum-sick."

"Don't you think, after all that exercise, we ought to have one more little drink?" Rusty Fergus asked wistfully.

Barnhorst's great laugh boomed out. "The Injun and me both got a bottle. The best Valley Tan that money can buy. Come on, let's hit that hayloft in Holladay's barn."

As they sauntered toward the stage station to get their bedrolls, Kiowa Kempter said quietly: "They'll be trying it again, them three sonsabitches."

"I sure hope so!" Kid Antrim said, with intense feeling.

"Next time I draw on them I'm going to start shooting," Jud Crater promised himself gravely.

Dan Ruylander nodded. "You and me both, Jud."

Five

At breakfast in the early morning, amid laughter over the swollen lacerated faces of Antrim and Fergus, old Jud Crater said: "Stage line takes a roundabout route but it can't be helped. Runs almost due north as far as Eagle Rock, maybe a hundred and twenty miles. Then swings back south and west along the plains of the Snake clear across southern Idaho. And north again up the western border till we cross into Oregon. You're going to get real sick of stage coaches, I guarantee."

38

They loaded their luggage and gear on the top deck and in the rear boot, maintaining a lookout for Silk Coniff and his friends. There were three other passengers booked besides themselves—two prospectors and a traveling salesman—and Dan Ruylander elected to ride on top with old Jud and young Antrim. The driver and shotgun guard regarded the Rafter crew with approval.

"Lot of holdups lately," remarked the driver. "We get jumped this trip, I guess Harrigan and me won't have to do all the fighting."

The coach was one of Ben Holladay's six-horse Concords slung on bullhide thoroughbraces. They took their positions and made ready for the start, the driver and guard on the box with the mailbags and express strongbox under their legs in the front boot. Dan and Jud and the Kid sat behind them on a wide deck seat, their carbines close at hand. Barnhorst, Kempter and Fergus occupied the carriage below with the drummer and the gold-hunters. With a blare of his brass horn, the driver kicked off the brake, cracked his long whip like a gunshot, and set the horse in motion. They rolled out of Ogden without sighting the Coniff trio, and rocked into the north toward the Idaho line.

The sun was just rising aflame over the Wasatch barrier, and casting long shadows across the landscape. The air was still cool and smelled of new grass and leaves and sage. Dan Ruylander liked it on top with the wind in his face and the vast broken wilderness spread about in springtime glory. Kid Antrim had a black eye, gashed cheek and puffed mouth, but even those souvenirs from last night's brawl did not spoil entirely his blond boyish good looks or dim his blithe spirit.

Jud Crater chewed his tobacco in brooding silence, except when he roused himself to point out landmarks along the way, but Antrim discovered fresh wonders on every side. The Kid was fascinated by the driver, a jehu of lordly arrogance, and the way he poured the silk over his six-horse team. Crawling forward to converse with the men on the box, the Kid returned grinning. "Seventeen-foot long with an eight-inch popper of cord silk on the end. Twelve strands of buckskin lash on a whalebone whipstock ferruled with silver. He can pick flies off the leaders without even touching horseflesh. What a man with that whip and them reins! Boy, I'd sure like to learn to drive a stage coach."

All day long they drove northward in the heat and dust, jolting and smashing over the ungraded road, with stops at swing stations to change horses and grab a bite to eat. The Bannock Range rolled along on the west, and the northernmost Wasatches marched against the eastern skyline. They made an overnight stop in Pocatello, on the Portneuf, and enjoyed baths and shaves and beds to sleep in once more.

At sunup they were on the highway again, and that second afternoon out of Utah they pulled into Eagle Rock. There Idaho Falls cascaded with a white-spumed roar into the deep canyon of the Snake River, and gulls from Great Salt Lake soared overhead in the fading sunshine. Jud Crater said the town got that name because an eagle had a nest on a huge rock that rose from the stream.

"We'll see a lot of the Snake, going out and coming back," Jud promised. "We're practically going to live with this river from here on, boys. And when we trail-drive the herd back, you'll have to work some real river crossings including a couple on the Snake. It's one of the damnedest rivers in the whole country. Rises in the Yellowstone of Wyoming, flowing south and then west in a great eight-hundred mile bend across Idaho. Turns north there and runs up some two-hundred miles more, forming the boundary between Idaho and Oregon and then between Idaho and Washington.''

Rusty Fergus gazed at him with awe. "You know everything, don't you, Jud?'

"Not quite, Red," said Jud Crater, leathery cheeks crinkling with his grin. "Just a little geography I learned from the old mountain men and checked on maps later. My father was one of 'em. He trapped with Jim Bridger and the rest of them old coots. You wouldn't believe how wild and tough they was. Grew men in them days. Outrun an antelope, outclimb a mountain goat, wrastle a grizzly, tear the fur off a bobcat. And drink enough liquor to flood the Big Muddy and overrun the Mississippi. They was more animal than human, more Injun than white, and the world will never see the likes of 'em again.''

"I was born too late, Jud," said Kid Antrim, shaking his golden head in mock gravity.

"Was you born in them days, Kid," said Jud Crater, "they would've thrown you back to feed the fishes.''

They saw nothing of Silk Coniff and his associates in Eagle Rock. The following day they started their southward-dipping arc west across Idaho Territory.

Below Idaho Falls, the stage road twisted along the Snake River Plains, a broad belt of sagebrush bottoms from fifty to seventy-five miles wide with mountain walls lifting along either side. The stream ran from several hundred to several thousand feet below the level of the plains, its gorges and falls spectacular in places. The plains had been built up in ancient times by lava sheets flooding down from the now extinct volcanos of the Craters of the Moon country to the north, according to old Jud Crater. "Maybe named by or after my old man," he added whimsically . . . . The flats were scarred with lava outcroppings and dykes, studded by angular desert buttes and shattered volcanic cones. Irrigation had been introduced in certain sections to support farms and ranches along the valley.

The next overnight stay was at American Falls. From there the road swerved northwestward, away from the Snake River itself but still on the plains, with the great mountain ranges—the Lost River, Lemhi and Beaverhead—tiered against the northern horizon.

Another sleeping stop at Shoshone, on the Little Wood, and still no sign of Coniff, Haydock and Klugstad. Perhaps they had shaken the gunmen, but Dan Ruylander was inclined to doubt it. Silk Coniff would be coming somewhere behind them, or maybe the three rustlers were on horseback and ahead of the stage coach by now.

The Concord crashed on toward Boise and the western boundary of Idaho, its passengers racked and beaten into a state of numb groggy exhaustion, and the serrated wall of the Sawtooth Mountains guarded the northern edge of the Snake River Plains here.

"They'll be building a railroad through this valley in a year or so," Jud Crater said. "The Oregon Short Line, I hear they're going to call it. The Northern Pacific is already building across the upper end of Idaho."

"The U.P. should've put a line in along the Snake," said Dan Ruylander.

"They'll take it over after the O.S.L. fails," Jud said cryptically. "Big business monopolies gobble up everything in this country nowadays. Old Rockefeller's showing 'em how to do it."

Six days and four hundred miles or more out of Ogden, Utah, they disembarked from the stage in Boise, a mining center and the territorial capital. It seemed as though they had been tossed about on that coach forever, and the Rafter men were ready for another barber-shop session of tub and chair and a good rest in comfortable hotel bedrooms.

The dining room menu included vegetables from the fertile Boise Valley, which drained into the Snake River, and they had their best meals of the journey there. Agricultural and livestock developments had followed the gold rushes, and were well advanced in this area of southwestern Idaho.

Eddie Foy, the New York comedian, was playing the Capitol Theater, up from a tour of the Southwest. The men from Wyoming took in the show and caught Foy's famous *Kalamazoo in Michigan* act. Afterward they encountered the little comic in the hotel barroom, and old Jud Crater fell in to talking with him about mutual acquaintances down in Kansas and Arizona. Foy said that Dodge was on the decline now. Wyatt Earp and his brothers, Doc Holliday, Luke Short, Bat Masterson, and other prominent figures known to Jud, had transferred to the new boomtown of Tombstone.

"It's even wilder than Dodge was—if that's possible," said Eddie Foy. "A man's crazy to step on the stage in that Birdcage Opera House. If I didn't have so many gunslinging friends down there, I'd have been torn to pieces and hung from the gallery in five minutes."

The conversation switched to politics and Foy said, "Somebody's going to kill President Garfield. That's not a joke, gentleman. A fortune-teller I know predicted it, and she never misses. I'd lay bets on it, but it wouldn't be sporting. A bit on the cold-blooded side too . . . . You know who the Vice President is? Well, don't feel bad. Nobody else does either."

Later that night, upstairs in the room with Jud Crater already in bed, Dan Ruylander sat by the window smoking his pipe and thinking. The nearer they drew to their objective, the more troubled was his mind. He dreaded meeting the Terrells and shrank from joining a blood-feud that had started six years before he was born. It didn't make much sense to him. Dan hoped

Garry and Sue Terrell would be easy to hate. He couldn't actually hate them for their dead parents' betrayal of his own father. Difficult to hate anyone you'd never seen.

The Pioneers on the Oregon Trail had bivouacked here at Old Fort Boise, established as an outpost of the Hudson's Bay Company in the fur-trading era. He tried to visualize Owen Terrell and Melinda encamped in this vicinity thirty years ago. Had they made love that night? Or had they been too preoccupied watching the back trail, living in fear of Dirk Ruylander overtaking them? Did it matter, now that they were both under the ground?

Well, it wouldn't be long now before Dan faced their children. One more day to the crossing of the Snake and Oregon soil. Two more days to Baker City, on a branch of the Powder, not far distant from the Terrells' Triangle . . . . It was odd that the girl Sadie had come from there; or perhaps she was just lying about it, as coached by Silk Coniff. The memory of her duplicity still irked him, heated his cheeks and ears with shame. Dan had been attracted to Sadie, and set up because of her pretended interest in him.

He wondered where Coniff and Haydock and Klugstad were tonight, and why they hadn't made another attempt at him. They couldn't have turned back. They wanted his life and the contents of his money belt too badly to relinquish their efforts. They'd strike again somewhere, either on the road or in Baker.

Dan Ruylander removed the dead pipe from his teeth and placed it on the table. He was through thinking and fretting, and ready to sleep—or try to. He wanted to believe that saying of Jud Crater's: "The thing a man worries the most about don't ever seem to happen." But it wasn't easy at twenty-four, with his burden of responsibility.

Six

The sun was lowering over the distant Cascade Range of Oregon, when the Concord coach approached the crossing of the Snake River in the late afternoon. The Rafter men were the only passengers now. It seemed to Dan Ruylander that they had worn out countless relays of horses, drivers and guards, travelers and vehicles. Only Rafter went on forever through scorching heat and choking dust, jounced and beaten about on hard horsehair cushions, with the reach-and-bolster crashing and gravel spattering underneath the floorboards.

The canyon walls were depressed into fairly low and gradual bluffs at this point south of Payette, where a cable ferry plied to and fro across the stream. The stage clattered out the dock onto the flat raftlike ferry, strung on twin cables attached to huge winches on either bank. The driver set his brake, tied his ribbons, and clambered down over the front wheel, as the shotgun guard dropped off the other side. The passengers got out to ease bruised bodies and sore limbs, and Jud Crater distributed Winchesters to them.

"Got a prickly feeling up my backbone," he explained dryly. "Maybe I'm just scared of the goddamn water, but it could be something else."

They drifted about the deck, stretching and yawning and enjoying this freedom of movement, as the windlasses began to creak and groan and the cables hauled the ferry away from the wharf on the Idaho shore. The current was quite strong, even in this comparatively calm stretch of the Snake, laying an insistent pressure against the great cumbersome float.

45

The cool breeze off the water was a blessed relief to men saturated in sweat and plastered with trail dirt. There was white water in midstream, surging against the ferry and straining the taut hawsers, until it seemed as if they must snap under the terrific tension.

"See what I mean about this river?" Jud Crater said, squirting a stream of tobacco juice overboard. "Feel the power of it, son?"

Dan Ruylander inclined his high tawny head. "If those wires gave, we'd sure take a ride, Jud."

Crater stared downstream to the north. "Rapids and falls below, Danny. This thing wouldn't last long."

Fergus and Antrim were talking nearby, carbines under their arms.

"Ain't it hell to be carted around the country like so many sacks of grain, Kid?" said Rusty. "I never want to see another goddamn stage coach, or a train neither."

"You said it, Red," drawled the Kid. "If I ever get back on a good horse again, I'm never going to get off. Breaking your butt in a christly Concord you're only halfway alive."

Dan Ruylander glanced toward the western bluffs, half-blinded by the low reddening sun. So that was Oregon, the land his father set out for and never reachd . . . . It didn't look any different, and probably wasn't until you got to the coast and the Pacific. Their destination was northeastern Oregon.

The ferry was shuddering and yawing on the vibrant lines, about two-thirds of the way across, when the first rifleshots cracked out at it from the Oregon landing. Bullets snarled and tore up showers of splinters, and the off lead horses reared with a scream and went down kicking in the traces. The driver sprang to hold the other lead horse's head and try to quiet the whole panicked team. The winches no longer turned and forward motion had ceased. They were caught like sitting ducks on a flat rock, with three or four rifles pouring it on them, the rapid windtorn reports floating out over the water.

"The sneaking sniping sonsabitches," Kid Antrim said, jacking a .44-40 cartridge into the chamber of his carbine.

The Rafter men and the stage guard had spread out with quick instinctive reaction, crouching, kneeling or lying prone on the deck to squint into the glaring sun and return that fire. The response from the stranded ferry was swifter and far stronger than the attackers had counted on, and the shooting from the shore slackened off perceptibly as those Wyoming Winchesters hammered away at the deck and winch-housing. The driver was still struggling to subdue his surviving lead horse and team, and everyone else on the raft was working a carbine. Empty brass shells glistened on the bleached wood.

"Get down!" Jud Crater called. "Flatten out, everybody. There ain't enough of 'em to hurt us much, the bushwhacking bastards."

Dan Ruylander dropped from his crouching position to the deck, and hitched his way forward to a better vantage point. The Coniff outfit must have taken over the Oregon landing, but they hadn't accomplished much more beyond killing one of Ben Holladay's horses . . . . Still, they've got us hung up and more or less helpless in mid-river, Dan reflected gloomily. They might pick us off in time, if we don't keep them pinned down pretty tight. I wish that damn sun would go down.

Dan reloaded his carbine and narrowed his eyelids against that dazzling crimson glare. They had it rigged all right, he thought. But they didn't wait quite long enough. If they'd pulled us in closer, they could have slaughtered us all . . . . Another burst of gunfire lashed out from the bluff, and Dan felt the breath of lead and the sting of splinters. He lined his sights and let go at the winking flashes and the powdersmoke, squeezing off, jacking the lever, aiming and firing again. Other Winchesters were blasting steadily all around him, and the shoreline rifles were stilled once more. The ferry had too much firepower for those three bushwhackers to combat.

"They couldn't shoot frigging fish in a barrel!" laughed Kid Antrim.

"They'll be trying something else," Kiowa Kempter warned gruffly.

A different chopping sound drifted out over the stream, and Rusty Fergus yelled: "They're doing something to them cables!"

The guide-wires were quivering with a new violence, Dan Ruylander observed, and the raft was bobbing and tilting with increased agitation. They might be using axes on that windlass. The notion chilled him to the bone . . . . Dan was slamming shots into the winch-house, when the cables parted with a muffled explosion. The lines recoiled, writhing like mammoth snakes, and threshed the water into a foaming boil as they sank beneath the surface. Cut loose and free, the ferry lurched into a crazy spin, whirling and rocking dizzily as the current caught it. Then they were borne downstream with sickening speed, and Dan had never felt so utterly futile and helpless.

"It ain't far to them rapids and falls!" shouted the guard, hoarse with terror. Loose cables rasped through iron brackets as the raft plunged along.

"Get out the ropes!" Jud Crater cried, and Barnhorst and Fergus mounted the coach to toss down lariats from the saddle gear.

"Never reach land with 'em," Kiowa Kempter prophesied. "Nothing to hang a loop on if we did."

"Splice 'em together, two by two," Jud said. "That'll give us a hundred feet or better to a line. We got to try something."

"We're swinging near the Oregon side," Kid Antrim declared.

"Still too goddamn far to throw a loop," muttered Barnhorst.

Dan Ruylander was already shedding his clothes, yanking off his gun belt and boots, flipping the wadded money belt to old Jud Crater. "I'll swim it with a couple of lines," he said. "Tie 'em around my waist, Barney, and make your ends fast here."

The severed cable ends had whipped clear of the ferry now and sunk lashing into the depths of fast water.

Jud clutched his bare arm. "You can't do it, Dan. Noboday can swim the Snake, for chrisake."

"I can, Jud. It's not too far now."

"Let somebody else go then."

Dan grinned. "I'm the best swimmer. You know that, Jud. Some of these boys can't swim a stroke."

"What the hell you going to snub the ropes on?" demanded Jud.

"Rocks, trees, I'll find something." Dan scanned the Oregon riverbank and bluffs, balancing himself against the pitch and sway of the runaway craft. Barnhorst secured the lines about Dan's naked body, and knotted the loose ends to ringbolts in the shoreward side of the ferry. It was no longer spinning as they gained momentum.

"They'll follow down and shoot you to ribbons," Jud Crater said. "Goddamnit, Dan, I can't let you do this! Old Dirk'll have my hide."

"Our best bet, Jud," said Dan Ruylander. "I'll make it okay."

The Snake had narrowed as it rampaged northward, between higher and sheerer walls with breaks here and there, and the raft was angling nearing the Oregon side. It was only about eighty feet to the boulder-strewn gravel beach, but the current was wicked, slashing and frothing around jagged rocks. It didn't look as if any

49

man could swim and live through that eighty-foot riptide of treacherous water.

"We'll cover you, Danny," said Barnhorst. "If them bastards ride down that rim, they'll run into plenty of lead."

Dan Ruylander took a running start and flung himself far out in a long flat dive, the lines trailing slackly behind him, the men on board watching with breathless anxiety and prayerful hope. The water smashed him with a silver-sprayed shock, and the current wrenched at him with incredible fury, rolling him over and under.

A rock jarred and raked him, and Dan hoped the ropes wouldn't get entangled down there. An undertow sucked him deep below the surface, tugging and clinging with remorseless suction, but somehow Dan thrashed and fought his way out of it. He climbed upward through endless rushing depths, his head and lungs bursting before he broke the surface and gulped air.

The river mauled and twisted him with giant strength, and Dan Ruylander had to fight and strain for every foot of headway. He was under water half the time, kicking and clawing to escape that tenacious undercurrent, and when he emerged the shoreline seemed as far away as ever. The flood catapulted him at a black boulder, and Dan jerked himself around barely in time to take the impact on his shoulder. He squirmed and crawled to the inner side of the rock, right shoulder and arm feeling crushed and numb.

Kicking off from the slimed stone, Dan lunged shoreward and slashed his way through another torrential expanse of the Snake. The beach *was* closer now, but the current still threatened to tear his limbs from his body, if it didn't drag him under and drown him first. His breath was gone, his sight and senses dimmed, and all the strength battered and drained from his rangy frame. He went on stroking, striving, fighting the river like a live enemy on nerve and will alone now.

At 'last the fury and the pressure eased somewhat. Dan Ruylander drove onward until he felt the sand and pebbles of the shallows under his palms and knees. Half-drowned and less than half-conscious, he floundered ashore and fell exhausted on the shelving gravel beach. It required an enormous effort for him to get up, undo the knots with numb shaking fingers, and lash the lines about a great imbedded boulder.

"There, by Jesus," Dan panted, almost falling on his agonized face.

Just in time too. In another minute or so the ferry would have been swept beyond the limit of the hundred-foot ropes, and Dan would have been hauled back to a watery death in the Snake River . . . . "Thank God," he sobbed, when he saw how close it had been. The lines anchored hard and fast below a bulge in the rock, Dan Ruylander collapsed panting in the dirt, while the men on the raft pulled themselves in toward the Oregon shore.

Dan hated to stir, even when the first bullets from the blufftop screeched off nearby stones and geysered the gravel around him. But he finally roused himself enough to worm his naked body into shelter. The men on the ferry cut loose with their carbines, and quickly drove the snipers above back from the rim of the palisade . . . . One of the ropes snapped before the ferry got in, but the other held until it was beached. The sound of friendly voices was welcome indeed to Dan.

Now they'd have to haul the raft along by hand, until they came to a break in the bluff which would permit the passage of the stage coach. But Dan Ruylander wouldn't be expected to share in that chore. Then they'd go into the little settlement of Ontario for the night . . . . Dan shivered and looked at the damp earth under his dripping face. The soil of Oregon, he mused. And what a way to get here, jaybird naked and half-dead. Well, I could have been fully dead. All of us, in fact . . . . We

51

almost didn't make Oregon, any more than Dad did in '51.

Another day and they'd be in Baker City. Then the real trouble would begin.

"Danny, you're one helluva swimmer," Kid Antrim said, bringing up his clothes and a towel. "Get that dirt off and I'll rub you down."

Dan Ruylander smiled faintly. "Tried to tell Jud that, Kid. But nobody believes a bragging man, I reckon."

"It was Coniff," said Antrim. "I spotted them sonsabitches on the rim."

The others rigged more tow lines while Dan reluctantly went back into the river to wash off the mud and a little blood from abrasions and scratches. Kid Antrim gave him a brisk, thorough rubdown with the rough towel, and Dan began to feel alive again. Kiowa Kempter broke out a bottle of whiskey to sterilize his cuts, and Dan took a deep swig of it, relishing the warm glow that spread inside him. The bottle was passed around until emptied, and Kiowa sent it skimming into the water with the remark, "They have firewater in Oregon, don't they?"

"Sure do, Injun," grinned Barnhorst. "We're still in America."

Jud Crater handed Dan the money belt. "Thought for a spell this was going to the bottom of the Snake, son. You pulled us out of that one, Danny."

The nearest break in the canyon wall was a short distance upstream. The men laid hold of the ropes and started hauling the heavy ferry along the shore, grunting and swearing under the strain. It was slow and killing work. Fortunately, the raft was free from the worst of the current. Barnhorst and Kempter utilized their great strength to advantage here. Dan dressed in a hurry and moved up the bank to lend a hand. It took every ounce they had to drag that ponderous burden. They paused and snubbed the lines frequently to rest.

"The old French *voyageurs* had one big rope they called the cordelle," Jud Crater said pantingly. "Used it mile after mile—up the Missouri."

"Only one goddamn way to travel," gasped Kid Antrim. "That's on a horse."

It was dark when they reached the opening in the wall and moored the ferry. Dan scouted the bluff with Antrim and Fergus, but found no trace of the enemy. The dead horse had been cut out of the harness, and the stage was ready to roll with only the driver aboard. The others had to push the vehicle from behind to get up the rough grade, but they finally made it after a sweating cursing ordeal in the darkness. "This is a trip to end all trips," Rusty Fergus mumbled.

After a nightmare cross-country ride that all but splintered their spines and jolted their teeth loose, they returned to the highway and reached Ontario. There was no hotel, but they made arrangements to bed down in the stage depot barn. There was a saloon, however. They found two ferry-men at the bar, nursing headaches and drowning their sorrow in redeye. The Rafter riders joined them with a will, and the Snake Crossing Saloon did a land-office business that night.

At dawn, weary and sick with hangovers, they piled back into the stage coach for the home stretch. Seventy-five miles to Baker City, and the end of the line for six travel-galled men from Wyoming . . . . Low in mind and spirits, his stomach quaking and his head splitting at every jolt of the wheels, Dan Ruylander felt certain that the worst was yet to come.

The last lap was slow and interminable. The sun sank behind the Blue Mountains, and the moon rose over the Rockies of Idaho. It was late, nearly midnight, when Kid Antrim's clear voice roused Dan in his rear corner seat, bulwarked by Barney's rawboned shoulder. "That must be Baker, boys. In full bloom at this hour." Dan Ruylander moaned and straightened up in misery, blinking at the lights with odd mingled emotions. He felt cold and empty with a premonition of disaster. Something told him that his fate and destiny—and perhaps his death—awaited him here.

The night life was still booming as they racked into town, and climbed from the stage for the last time with infinite relief. Unloading and stacking their gear in the depot, they repaired to the Powder Horn Saloon to quench a long thirst and make inroads on the free-lunch counter. Along the bar men were talking about Paddy Ryan who had won the bare-knuckle heavyweight championship of the world last year from English Joe Goss, and a challenger from Boston named John L. Sullivan.

Too tired to linger, the Rafter riders gathered up their luggage, hired three double rooms in the Great Northwest House, and went to bed at once. But weary as he was, Dan Ruylander lay awake for some time after Jud Crater was deep in slumber . . . . Dan missed his father, his brother and sister, and the ranch. He was lonesome, sad and homesick as a wet-eared kid. Wyoming seemed as distant as the lofty white moon he could see through the fly-specked window. He wished old Dirk had cancelled out this ancient score and let them stay at home on the Sweetwater.

Seven

When Dan woke Jud was gone and the sun told him it was midday or thereabouts. He lay back and tried to sleep some more, but it eluded him. He was sitting on the edge of the bed scratching the bronze stubble on his jaws, when big Barnhorst and Kiowa Kempter came in carrying a large tub of steaming water. They had bathed, shaved, and changed from filty rumpled store clothes into clean range garb. They looked so fresh and healthy that Dan groaned at the sight of them.

"This is for being a hero the other day, Danny," said Barnhorst. "Extra special de luxe service, only for the brave."

"Warmer than the Snake, Dan," said Kempter. "No current neither."

"This is too much," Dan Ruylander said. "But I sure appreciate it."

"No, it ain't too much," Kempter said solemnly. "I never learnt how to swim, Dan."

"I'm no hand at it neither," Barnhorst admitted sheepishly.

Dan dipped out a basin full of water and started lathering up to shave while the tub cooled a little. "I thought all Injuns swam, Kiowa."

"I'm only a quarter red, Dan."

The door opened again, as Dan finished razoring and rinsed off the soap, and Rusty Fergus and Kid Antrim entered with a pot of coffee and a plate of sandwiches, cream, sugar and a cup. They too were barbered and immaculate in riding clothes, bright and shining clean.

"For our savior," Fergus said. "Breakfast in bed—almost."

"Snake River Ruylander he was known as, from that day on," said Antrim, pouring the coffee and adding sugar and cream.

Dan smiled at them, with a catch in his throat. "I don't know what to say, boys." The Kid told him to shut up and eat then, and Dan discovered that he was hungry as he devoured a sandwich of roast beef, washed down with the strong coffee. Getting into the bathrub, he relaxed with luxurious ease in the soothing warmth, while the others lounged or sauntered around smoking and chatting. Suddenly the strange sunlit room had become friendly and homelike, a pleasant place to be. Glowing all over, Dan went to work with the soap.

Jud Crater made his entrance, fresh from the full treatment in a barber shop and smoking a long thin cigar, as Dan Ruylander was getting into a clean outfit of range clothing. "I wonder how the poor folks are getting along these days," Jud commented dryly, watching Dan pause for another bite of sandwich and drink of coffee. Feeling wonderfully restored and renewed, Dan plucked a cigar from the pocket of Jud's buckskin vest and bit off the end. Jud flicked a match on his thumbnail and held the light for Dan, drawling: "Allow me, Your Highness." Dan grinned through fragrant blue smoke and finished combing his damp sun-streaked hair.

They trooped downstairs and out through the lobby to sit on the long gallery with their boots on the heel-gouged railing, aware of the slight animosity the natives showed to strangers from the outside. Oregon had been a state in the Union since 1859, and its citizens regarded people from the territories as wild and uncivilized.

Baker City was a lively center for stock-raising, mining and freighting interests, with agriculture developing since the advent of irrigation. The business section, with its false fronts and board awnings, slat walks and hitch-rails, looked much like any frontier community. Miners and farmers were more or less the same everywhere, but there was a marked difference in the riding men out here. The same difference that Dan had noticed in Utah and Idaho. The far west followed the customs of California, whereas Wyoming and Montana held to the traditions of Texas and the Southwest.

"Take their riding," Jud Crater said. "They use single-cinch rigs and set leaning back with their stirrups forward, where we ride straight up and down. They dally their ropes instead of tying to the horn. They sling their guns higher than we do, and their hats are high-crowned with narrow curled-up brims. Look at them heavy saddle-horns and that big spade bit they use. Their reins are closed where ours are split, and their head stalls are light and fancy while ours are heavy and plain.

"Everything's different out here. They even talk different. They call their main herd the parada, and their horse herd a cavvy instead of a remuda. They call their riders buckaroos and their mavericks orejanas instead of slicks. They're in the same business we are, but they do everything different."

"They don't look like much to me," Kid Antrim declared.

"They're pretty good cattle men, Kid," said Jud Crater. "You'll find that out as time goes on here."

"Crazy to ride them single-rigs," Rusty Fergus said. "And how in hell can they make a quick draw with them irons halfway up to their armpits?"

"I don't know how but they do it, Redhead," said Jud. "This Hawk Fallon from Triangle shot a fella when I was out here last summer. Real good and fast, about as fast as anything I ever saw. And they claim young Terrell's just as good or better than the Hawk."

"Has Triangle got any strong-arm boys, Jud?" asked Barnhorst.

"They got two cut to order for you and the Injun, Barney. A pair of grizzlies named Pike Urbom and Otis Sowerby."

Barnhorst laughed easily. "Don't even like their names."

"You'll like their faces even less," Jud Crater told him.

They loafed around all afternoon, looking the town over and watching for the Coniff party, drinking beer and shooting pool. "It's a pleasure just to stay put for a while," Dan Ruylander said. "When I got in bed last

57

night I could still feel the grinding of that stage coach."

"Old Jud was probably snoring enough to shake the bed apart," Kid Antrim grinned.

"Not me, button," said Crater. "I sleep very genteel."

Baker City was on the south fork of the Powder River, which flowed eastward into the Snake River Canyon. The Blue Mountains formed the western skyline, and to the north was the granite and marble upthrust of the Wallowas, with sharp peaks attaining an altitude of 10,000 feet. Southward lay the great basin area, stretching down to the Nevada border. Alkaline lakes, shallow and shrinking in the dry season, occupied troughs between the fault-block mountains of the basin, and the streams in this region dwindled through evaporation or seepage.

The Rafter crew had supper in the dining room of the Great Northwest House, and wandered around the evening streets to digest the food. It was gratifying to be free from schedules and timetables, trains and stages, with leisure hours to spend as they wished.

They were sitting about a rear corner table in the Powder Horn, when a man entered with the announcement: "Triangle's in town." His words seemed to put a sudden constraint on the customers, even the drunker ones. It was evident that Triangle commanded fear and respect in Baker. Several men departed and others endeavored to make themselves small and scarce in the smoke-layered barroom. Dan Ruylander and his riders waited with calm watchful interest.

Triangle came in with a swagger, spreading out inside the batwings to survey the interior with mild contempt. Big lean tough men in better clothing than most cowhands wore, their hats and belts, holsters and boots plainly expensive. Around him Dan could feel the instinctive bristling of his Rafter crew, and Dan himself felt a stir and surge of antagonism. Perhaps it wouldn't be so hard to hate the Terrell outfit, after all.

"That's Hawk Fallon in the lead," Jud Crater murmured, as the Oregon men moved with lazy arrogance to the bar.

"Cocky bunch of bastards," remarked Kid Antrim, with extreme distaste on his keen boyish features.

"Almost as cocky as you and Red," agreed Jud dryly, and went on to identify some of the others. "The squat ugly one with the shaghead is Otis Sowerby. The thin dark man with the wild-bronc look they call Chill Cahoon. That giant showing his tusks like a boar is Pike Urbom. The slick dapper dandy goes by the name of Vern Winslett. I disremember the rest, but them first five are the bad ones."

"They look it all right, Jud," said Dan Ruylander. "Where's Garry Terrell?"

"He don't mix much with the common herd, Danny."

Dan nodded with a slow smile. It was easy enough to dislike these Triangle hands at first glance. Maybe it was going to be just as simple and natural to hate Garry Terrell, too. Dan hoped so. It would make his mission a whole lot easier and more satisfying.

Hawk Fallon was tall and well-built, the hair under his rakish hat darkly auburn. Strange amber eyes burned palely from his proud fierce face, and the scornful smile reminded Dan a little of Silk Coniff. But Fallon was the more dangerous, Dan figured, a formidable character in any company. It showed in the elastic ease of Fallon's movements, the insolent assurance of his manner. A killer, and proud of it. That was Hawk Fallon.

"Let's be going, boys," Dan Ruylander said. "We don't want to tangle with them—yet."

As Rafter moved toward the doorway, the Triangle men turned from the bar to look them over. Hawk

59

Fallon lifted a languid hand and said: "Howdy, strangers. What's your hurry?"

"No hurry." Dan swung around to face him, and they measured one another in cool silence, Dan's gray eyes meeting the yellow ones steadily. Fallon was an inch or so taller than Dan's six-one height, an older man by several years perhaps, with more self-assurance than Dan had ever encountered.

"Where you from? East or south?" Fallon asked, breaching Western etiquette with pleasant even tones.

Dan decided to ignore the impoliteness, and said: "Wyoming."

"After cattle?"

"That's right."

"Triangle's overstocked with the best shorthorns and white-faces in the country," Hawk Fallon said, taking it for granted that Triangle and himself were known to everybody. "You'll want to see Garry Terrell in the morning."

"Maybe I will," Dan Ruylander conceded indifferently, turning away toward the batwings. Rafter trailed after him, exchanging cold glances with the Triangle men as they passed, and Hawk Fallon watched them all the way out with casual contempt.

Outside on the plank walk, Kid Antrim laughed softly. "The kingpins of Powder River for sure. This is liable to be more fun than I figured, Danny."

"Don't underrate 'em too much, Kid," warned Jud Crater. "They're almost as tough as they act."

"Nobody could be *that* tough, Jud!" scoffed Rusty Fergus.

They strolled along to the front of the Great Northwest, and Dan said: "I've got to write Dad tonight, and I'd better get at it." He was still dry-mouthed and quivering a little inwardly from the meeting with Hawk Fallon and Triangle. There was another man he'd have to fight someday. Dan felt it as

60

strongly as he had with Silk Coniff . . . . Fallon, like Coniff, was an enemy to the death. The current of hatred was there the instant they laid eyes on one another. And Dan hoped it would spring up again when he met Garry Terrell. Maybe tomorrow.

"I'll ride herd on these outlaws, Dan," said Jud Crater. "Go write your letter."

There was writing material in the room. Dan lighted the lamp and settled down to the chore. He was fairly well educated for his time and environment, thanks to his mother and father and Jud Crater, but letter-writing was an unaccustomed task that set him to frowning. In a neat angular hand, he wrote:

Baker City, Oregon
June 5th, 1881

Dear Dad & All:

Just a line to let you know we got here safe and sound, about midnight last night. Saw some of the Triangle riders tonight, and expect to meet the Terrells tomorrow. All hands are well and everything is going fine.

The trip out was long and rough, but we saw a lot of new country. And learned a lot from old Jud, who is better than any teacher I ever had in school. Coniff and his friends were on the train, and I expect they're out here somewhere now. Had a little brush with them in Ogden, and another when we crossed the Snake River into Oregon, but nobody got hurt at all.

This looks like good country, but I'll still take Wyoming. Miss you and the kids, and Rafter and the Sweetwater. But I'm lucky to have Jud and the other boys with me. You couldn't ask for a better crew, Dad.

Hope all is well with you and Judith and Hud and the ranch. Don't worry about us. We'll make out all right, and get home with the herd early in the fall.

Saw the famous NY comedian Eddie Foy in

Boise. He told Jud that Wyatt Earp and others you know had left Dodge and gone to Tombstone, Arizona, which is booming. He was pretty funny.

Maybe I'll hold this until I meet Terrell. Wanted to get it started tonight anyway, but there isn't much to say. It has been a great trip, Dad. Out here they dress and ride and pack their guns kind of funny, but Jud says they're good cattle men. We've had a lot of fun and expect to have more, along with some hard work.

That's all for now. More later probably. Best to you all from all of us out here . . . .

With a sigh of relief, Dan Ruylander addressed an envelope and placed the folded letter inside, leaving the flap unsealed. There was no sense in mailing it until after he saw Garry Terrell and had some real news to report. Corresponding this way wasn't very satisfactory, but it was better than losing contact altogether.

Dan smoked a pipeful of tobacco and began to get restless. It was too early to go to bed, after having slept until noon today. He got up and buckled on his gun belt again and slipped into a denim brush jacket, deciding to go out and kill some time with the boys until he got sleepy. Putting on his flat-crowned wide-brimmed hat, Dan blew out the lamp and stepped into the second-floor corridor.

He was almost at the head of the staircase, when a door creaked open and a feminine voice reached out to him: "Dan! Dan Ruylander, come here." Whirling smoothly, hand on gun, he saw the coppery head and sharp features of the girl called Sadie in a nearby doorway.

Dan lifted his Colt from the leather and eased back in the hammer. "If you've got Silk Coniff in there, he'd better start shooting—or running."

"There's nobody here but me, Dan," said Sadie. "Come on in. Quick, before somebody sees you! I don't want to get thrown out of this dump."

"Sure, I'm a sucker," Dan Ruylander murmured. "But if you're lying this time, baby, you'll catch the first one. Right in the teeth."

Eight

Dan inspected the room and closet and slid the .44 back into its sheath, while the girl locked the door behind him. Her perfume filled the place, subtle rather than sharp and feeding the natural hunger in him. Sadie was fastidious about her person, and the room was neat and orderly in the mellow lamplight. The drawn shades shut out the night world, leaving them in quiet isolation. She wore a dark green dress trimmed with white, and looked nicer than she had in the sleek satin gown in Ogden. He guessed that she wore a lot of green to go with her eyes.

"Where are your friends?" Dan asked bluntly.

"What friends?"

"Don't stall. You've got some explaining to do, Sadie. Old Jud was right about you back in Utah. And I was wrong."

Sadie shook her head. "No, you weren't, Dan. I really fell for you. You don't realize what a sweet good-looking boy you are."

Dan Ruylander laughed. "Don't give me that! I saw you let Coniff in the back door, after that brawl in the street."

"I made the deal with him before I saw you, Dan, or knew anything about you. I wanted to get back here, and Silk offered me the chance. I—I just can't travel alone." She sank into a chair. "I was coming to warn you that night in the Gold Nugget, when the fight broke out in the street. Because after I saw you, Dan, nothing else mattered.''

''Don't keep throwing that line, Sadie. Where are Silk and the other two now?''

''I don't know. But they're around here some place. And they'll be after you again.''

''You came with them, didn't you?'' Dan said. ''Talk straight for once.''

''As far as Boise,'' confessed Sadie, bowing her head and tapping a finger on her crossed knee. ''We cut across country to Shoshone Falls on horseback and got ahead of you. I knew they were going to jump you at the Ontario ferry, so I broke away from them in Boise. Thought I might get a chance to see you and warn you—but I didn't.''

Dan Ruylander paused in his pacing to shape and light a cigarette. ''It's a good story, Sadie. You'll forgive me if I don't quite believe it?'' His smile was ironic. This girl had been on his mind ever since Ogden, Utah. He'd wanted her, even after finding that she was in league with Silk Coniff . . . . ''What brought you back to Baker City? A man?''

''I don't really know, Dan,'' she sighed. ''There was a man—once. But I'll never see him again. Could be *you* brought me up here. Did you ever think of that?''

His grin was wry and sorrowful. ''Please, Sadie. I'm not as young and simple as you may think . . . . Are you going to work one of the honkytonks? Or set up business for yourself? Likely spot here by the head of the stairs.''

Sadie rose in one swift motion, her hand flashing hard and loud against his weathered brown cheek. She struck with sufficient force to rock his blond head and sting deeply. Dan started to reach for her but checked herself. ''All right, kid,'' he said slowly. ''I guess I asked for that one. Sorry, Sadie.''

Her green eyes brimmed with sudden tears, and she fell back in the chair rubbing the palm of her hand.

"Pour the drinks, will you please?" She indicated a bottle of brandy and two glasses on the stand. "And then get the hell out of here! I've got a little pride left, mister. I haven't always been a bum."

"I know it, Sadie. Anybody could see that. I said I was sorry." Glad of something to do with his hands, Ruylander uncorked the bottle and splashed out two substantial drinks. He tried to think of Sadie as a fellow human being instead of a woman. That way he could sympathize with her. But when he handed her the glass and saw her perky provocative features and lushly curved figure she was woman, ripe and desirable, and all Dan could do was want her with a primitive driving need.

"What's your last name?" he inquired, over the glass rim.

"What difference does it make? You can go now, Mr. Ruylander."

"I like to know people by their full names. Makes them more real."

"McLain," she said, and then with a grimace: "Oregon Sadie McLain. Is that full and real enough for you, Wyoming?"

Dan Ruylander leaned on the brass rail at the foot of the bed and sipped his brandy. "Who was the man here, Sadie?"

"He's dead as far as I'm concerned. Or rather I'm dead so far as he's concerned. Nobody you know anyway."

"What's Silk Coniff to you?"

"You ask a lot of questions, boy. But that one's easy to answer. Nothing, Dan, nothing whatever. No man has meant anything to me since I left this valley. Until I saw you walk into that dive in Ogden."

"Let's not have any more of that stuff, Sadie."

"Get out then!" she flared. "Nobody's got a rope on you. Beat it, cowboy!"

65

"Any folks, Sadie?" His voice was soft and gentle.

Her head turned slowly from side to side, shimmering like reddish bronze in the rays from the lamp. "Dead—as far as I know. Will you please go now? I don't want to cry again, goddamn it!"

"Too bad," Ruylander murmured, as if to himself.

"Don't feel sorry for me, damn you!" cried Sadie McLain. "Take the door. Get out and leave me alone. I mean it. I don't want you here. Go on back to that dried-up bowlegged little old godfather of yours, sonny."

"All right, Sadie." He set the glass down, picked up his hat, and started for the door. He was reaching for the knob and key, when she called, "Dan! Wait, Dan. . ." The words seemed involuntary, wrung from her anguished scarlet lips.

Dan Ruylander turned and saw that she had risen and was moving toward him like a sleep-walker. He took a long stride and Sadie flew at him. They met with a grinding rush, arms locked and clutching intensely, bodies molded from breast to knee. She tilted her coppery head back and raised her drawn eager face. Dan lowered his mouth to the sweet fullness of hers. Time ceased to exist as they swayed there, crushed close and breathless. Her fragrance and the firm soft warmth of her rioted through his senses. Flame erupted with pure white heat to weld and consume them. There was love and hate and lust in their embrace.

Then Sadie was straining to free herself, writhing and shoving at him as she moaned: "No, Dan, no! I'm no good—for you. It's too late, Dan. Let me go."

But Dan couldn't have released her, even if he'd wanted to. It had gone beyond that, and it didn't matter in this moment what she was or had been . . . . "I don't care, Sadie. You and I. What else is there?" he said, soft and fierce, holding her tight.

Sadie's arms gripped him once more, her face lifting

to his with intolerable rapture and torment. "You want me, Dan? No matter what?"

"God, yes!" he breathed, awed and wondering and helpless in this bursting floodtide of emotion. Dan hadn't known it could be like this with a girl. It never had been before.

"I'm yours, Dan," said Sadie McLain, frank and open and holding nothing back. No feminine coyness here. "I have been since the first time I saw you. You wouldn't believe me, Dan, but it's true."

Hours later when Dan Ruylander walked to his room like a man in a trance, Jud Crater was undressing there with the chew of tobacco still lumping the withered leather of his cheek.

"You stink of cheap perfume," Jud said acidly. "Don't tell me you went into a fancy house with that money belt on you? Godalmighty, boy, what are you thinking of?"

"I didn't go to any fancy house, Jud."

"You picked up some stray slut then, which is even worse. Maybe I'd better carry that money until we meet Terrell and get it into the bank."

"I didn't take any chances, Jud," insisted Dan patiently. "Quit fretting about me, will you?"

"Who was it, Dan?" demanded Crater, an angry little gray bantam in his underwear. "Where was you? Hellfire and brimstone, this ain't no goddamn picnic we're on!"

Dan was silent, stripping off his jacket and unbuttoning his shirt. Jud raked him with pale squinted eyes. "Damned if you don't act like a lovesick punk. All we need is for you to go overboard for some cheap little chippie. Coniff and his christly coyotes are skulking around hereabouts, and Triangle is primed and loaded for bear. And you're walking around like a moonstruck bull calf with his first smell of heifer."

"Lay off, Jud," said Dan wearily.

"I will like hell. Who was the woman?"

"She's all right. And I'm getting too old to be wet-nursed."

Jud Crater stared and wagged his grizzled head. "Lord in His Mercy help us all! I do believe that red-haired hellion from Utah has followed us up here. If she has, kid, it's to set you up for Silk Coniff . . . . Is she in Baker? Was it her?"

"Maybe so, Jud," said Dan Ruylander, with icy restraint. "Maybe she's here—and in love with me."

"Love? A girl of the line like that?" Crater groaned, as if in mortal pain. "She wants a share of that sixty thousand, you idiot. Women like her don't love nothing but money, for chrisake!"

"That's enough, Jud."

"You're in love with her too?" Cackling with mirthless laughter, Crater tossed his chew out the window and crawled into bed. "You had to come all the way out to Oregon to fall in love with a honky-tonk gal. Christ at the crossroads! Hope I sleep good and sound tonight, Danny. If I should wake up and get a whiff of you, I'd think sure I was back east in the biggest whorehouse in St. Louis."

Dan Ruylander had to grin, in spite of himself. "I hope you sleep sound too, you ornery old galoot. It's the only thing that shuts up that miserable mouth of yours. Don't you ever get tired of chewing my ears and peeling the hide off me, Jud?"

"Not when you deserve it, Dan, and that's most of the goddamn time," Jud Crater said. "But you can't tell a young'un nothing. That's one of the saddest things in the sorry world. You can't even tell 'em that fire is hot, until they get their tails burnt good and plenty."

Nine

In the morning Jud Crater returned from an early breakfast to wake Dan and say: "The Terrells are in town. Better get up, boy."

"Where are the boys?" Dan asked, blinking drowsily and yawning.

"Out and around," said Jud. "Playing pool ain't as wearing as some other pastimes I might mention."

Dan Ruylander shaved and washed and dressed with care, no longer so reluctant to meet Garry and Sue Terrell. He felt as if last night had matured and balanced him, given him added poise and confidence. Whatever Sadie McLain was, she had been what Dan needed at that time. Combing his tawny cropped hair, Dan thought he actually looked a little different in the cracked watery mirror. Less boyish and more like a man maybe. But it was probably just his imagination. The scent of Sadie still lingered faintly, stirring up memories and an inner shudder of desire. She was a lot of woman, regardless of what old Jud said about her.

They left the room and descended the stairway. A big rangy man in a well-tailored suit of rich gray flannel stood before the wide lobby window, and Dan sensed that it was Terrell even before Jud elbowed him. Garry Terrell turned from the window, strikingly handsome with crisp curly black hair and deep expressive brown eyes. He must look as his father had in youth, Dan reflected. His smiling recognition of Crater had all the warm spontaneous charm that Dirk had described as being Owen Terrell's chief stock in trade. But there'd been a rank rotten streak in Owen, and no doubt it had

69

been reproduced in his son.

Striding lithely forward, Terrell shook hands with Crater, and then with Dan, as Jud introduced them. "Glad to see you again, Crater," he said. "And I've been looking forward to meeting you, Ruylander. Heard you were in town. You'll both have breakfast with me, I hope. Been fighting off my appetite so we could eat together."

Dan agreed, and Jud said, "Had mine, but I'll take some more coffee with you."

In the hotel dining room it was obvious that the management spared no efforts to please Garry Terrell and his guests. The pancakes were light and crisp, the ham and eggs and fried potatoes done to perfection, and the coffee seemed better than they had tasted here previously. The service equalled that of Denver's fabulous Windsor.

"My sister Sue's still sleeping," Terrell explained. "We got in late last night. But she'll be down before long."

They talked about the trip out, cattle and horses and ranching problems, politics and business in general. Terrell was a most agreeable host and companion, and Dan saw that it was going to be difficult to dislike the young man. His friendly winning manner seemed wholly genuine and sincere, and he revealed none of the arrogance that marked his Triangle riders. On the contrary, Garry Terrell acted natural and unpretentious, almost naively simple and honest. But knowing his background, Dan Ruylander was far from convinced.

"Six of you, eh?" Terrell mused. "You'll need at least six more riders then, and about eight horses to a man. I'll see that you get top hands, and I know you'll like these big claybank geldings of ours. Wish I could make the drive with you myself. Always wanted to go back over the old Oregon Trail. My folks came out here

70

with a wagon train, you know. Back in 1851."

Dan nodded soberly, the long-distilled bitterness rising and rankling inside him. *Sure, they came out here,* he thought. *With my father's wagon and oxen, horses and bull and cows. With all my dad's money, his lifetime savings, leaving him flat broke and drugged half-to-death in old Fort Laramie . . . .* But apparently the younger Terrells knew nothing about that. It was understandable. Owen Terrell's side of the story was not one that a father would hand down to his children. This should give Dan a certain advantage in dealing with Triangle.

"I want to get to a bank," Dan Ruylander said. "I'm worn out from carrying all this money around."

"I'll take you as soon as the bank opens," offered Terrell. "Your check would have been acceptable, if you could have known it. After meeting Crater last summer, I made enough inquiries to learn that Rafter's as good as gold.

"We'll have you folks out to Triangle, of course," he continued, in smooth cultured tones. "You can set up camp on the North Powder, and hand-pick your own beef, if you want to. We've got horses for you too, and I'll get you a fair buy on wagons and equipment and provisions."

"That's sure nice of you, Terrell," said Dan. "We'll be much obliged for everything."

"Nothing at all, Ruylander." He gestured lightly. "Just good business for both sides. There's cattle here from the Grande Ronde and the John Day. From the Willamette and the coast, and as far away as Whatcom County on Puget Sound up in Washington. Too much stock for the grass. We're happy to have the Wyoming market opening up for us."

"We can use it back home," Jud Crater said. "No more longhorns coming up the trail."

"These Durhams and Herefords are way ahead of·

Texas longhorns," Garry Terrell declared. "Dual purpose, fine for both beef and milk. Just what you need for a native stock in Wyoming."

"They aren't as tough as longhorns though, are they?" asked Dan.

"Maybe not. But they're tough enough to stand a thousand-mile drive, and they won't lose too much tallow on the road, either."

By the time cigars were lighted over final cups of coffee, they were quite friendly at the table, comfortably at ease with one another. It was practically impossible to dislike Terrell, at this early stage anyway. He seemed as regular and congenial as a man could be, and he had a rare and disarming personal charm. Dan had always wondered how Dirk could have been duped so thoroughly by Owen Terrell. Now he knew. Garry was already like an old friend.

The coffee drained, they adjourned to front-porch chairs, to smoke their cigars and watch the huge freighters lumber past with dust swirling up into the morning sunshine. There were ox-teams of six and even nine yokes, dragging two or three heavy-laden wagons. There were six-horse and six-mule drays, and the incredibly long 12-span strings of the jerk-line skinners, who rode on the near wheel horse to guide their cumbersome outfits.

Up the street in front of the Powder Horn Saloon, Dan observed that the other four Rafter hands had once more encountered Triangle, the latter force numbering eight or nine today. They were all talking freely this morning, motioning toward ponies at the tie-racks and arguing heatedly about something.

"Our boys seem to be getting acquainted over there," remarked Garry Terrell.

"Yeah, but they ain't exactly getting friendly," Jud Crater said dryly. "Reckon I better drift along that way and keep the peace." He got up with a sigh and stalked off bowlegged, a wiry little man, hard as flint-rock and resilient as rawhide.

"Great old-timer there," Terrell said, glancing after Crater. "Hope our boys don't get to fighting. I guess my crew is a little salty. No doubt yours is too, Dan."

Ruylander smiled. "They're all of that. I suppose the sight of those center-fire rigs set 'em off."

"Must be it. I know they can't see anything but rimfire saddles in your country and the Southwest."

"We figure the single-cinch won't hold up under hard bucking or roping."

"It works out pretty well for us," Terrell said.

"Isn't it apt to cause sores?"

"Not if the saddle-blanket's arranged properly. We don't get any more sores than you double-rig men do."

"They're arguing ropes now," Dan said, grinning to cover his uneasiness. "We can't see burning our fingers off taking dallies on the horn."

Terrell chuckled. "And we don't believe in breaking our necks by tying hard-and-fast to the horn."

Dan Ruylander laughed. "Well, let's let them argue it out, Garry. I feel too good for a debate, with that fine breakfast under my belt and this cigar burning just right."

"Agreed, Dan," laughed Terrell. "Those arguments never get anywhere. It's as bad as arguing religion . . . . Here's Sue now." He rose with effortless grace, a new and tender quality lighting his dark eyes and clean features. Standing up with him Dan turned and froze, as he saw the girl walking toward them. He would have known Sue Terrell anywhere, he thought irrationally. She resembled the picture in that ancient gold locket his father still treasured. It tightened Dan's throat, chilled his spine, and set up a wild hollow thrumming in his chest. He was glad he'd had his suit cleaned and pressed.

Garry Terrell presented his sister, and Dan could

scarcely acknowledge the introduction. He had never been so moved by a girl's presence. Sue had a gracious ease of manner similar to her brother's. She was tall for a woman, slim and willowy with a ripe depth at breast and hip. Burnished black hair was drawn back from the flawless brow, and clear blue eyes regarded him with frank interest. Her skin was tanned to a golden brown.

Sue's nose was too prominent, her mouth too broad and full for prettiness, and the cheekbones and jaws stood out slightly. Handsome was the word that fitted her best. The beauty, if there was any, lay in the bone structure of her face. A sculptured look enlivened by some inner glow. She moved and stood like a young queen. There was both pride and humility in her. If Melinda was like this, Dan could comprehend what the loss had meant to his father. And why Owen Terrell had gone to such ends and depths to gain her for his own.

At the time Dan had no idea what she wore. Later he would recall her in a divided doeskin skirt, handmade riding boots, and a soft gray shirt. Something passed between them, almost a flicker of recognition, as if they had known one another well somewhere. In another life perhaps . . . . Ridiculous, but the fact remained that they *knew* one another instantly. This was no casual meeting. They were held in a strange spell of awed wondering and mute groping.

The brother and sister were chatting with light good fellowship, but Dan didn't hear them until Sue said: "I must go in to breakfast. I'm very sorry I was late, Mr. Ruylander." She eyed him with approval and appreciation that might have seemed bold in another woman. "But I'll see you later—I trust."

Dan Ruylander nodded, still unwilling to trust his tongue, and Garry Terrell said: "If we aren't here we'll be at the bank. Wait for us, Sue."

"I will," she promised. "And Garry—let's go back to Wyoming with them. We deserve a vacation."

"It wouldn't be exactly a vacation, Sue," said Terrell, smiling indulgently. "A thousand-mile trail drive with three thousand head. We'd have to work our way."

"I wouldn't mind that. Think of the country we'd see, Garry. We've always talked about retracing the Oregon Trail, and I'd like to see Wyoming."

"Well, there's plenty of time, Sue."

"Perhaps Mr. Ruylander wouldn't want us?"

"He sure would," Dan said, recovering some of his composure under the warm flattery of those blue eyes and wide smiling lips. Sue had a delightful way of crinkling her eyes when she smiled or laughed.

She left them with a gay salute, and the two men resumed their seats on the gallery. "Some girl," Terrell said, with boyish enthusiasm. "A real partner to me, Dan. I couldn't run Triangle without her."

"She's fine, Garry," agreed Dan, and thought that was putting it very mildly. He wished now he hadn't become involved with Sadie McLain last night. It made him feel vaguely ashamed, soiled and tainted and unworthy . . . . Then he remembered who Sue Terrell was, and what her parents had done his father, and the true purpose behind this mission to Oregon. He'd better forget about Sue Terrell and stay with Sadie—if he had to have a woman out here.

But Sue knew me, he thought dismally. *Just as I knew her.*

Jud Crater rejoined them and reckoned there wouldn't be any bloodshed in the street, at least not for the time being. "They can't get together on how a saddle ought to be rigged or a six-gun packed, or what kind of rope is best and whether it should be tied or dallied. But I doubt if they'll start throwing fists or guns over any of them burning issues."

Garry Terrell pointed to a man entering the Land and Cattle Bank of Baker County, diagonally across on the

75

opposite side of the street from the Great Northwest House. "There's our banker, Dan, if you want to see him now."

"The sooner, the better," Dan murmured, anxious to get rid of his burden of cash. In anticipation of an early visit to the bank, he had transferred the bills from the money belt to the inner breast pocket of his suit coat.

"I'll wait here and keep an eye on the boys and things," Jud Crater drawled. "In hopes that your sister'll come out, Garry, and give me something these old eyes can rest on with real pleasure."

They went down the steps, Dan Ruylander and Garry Terrell, and slanted across the churned dust in the direction of the buff brick structure that housed the bank. Two fine-looking boys, Jud Crater thought, watching them from the veranda. About of a size, tall and loose and easy, Dan fair and Terrell dark . . . . *Are they going to have to fight and maybe kill each other, because old Dirk Ruylander either couldn't or wouldn't forget a thirty-year-old-grudge?*

A lot of men might get shot and killed before this was over, Jud reflected morbidly. And for what? It wouldn't help old Dirk back there on the Sweetwater, any more than it would hurt those two lying in their graves at Triangle. Jud Crater swore softly and squirted an amber arc of tobacco juice over the porch rail. Life was just too goddamned much, at times.

Ten

The morning sun was still low and blood-red above the peaks of Idaho, paving the east-west avenues of Baker with ruddy gold, firing the eastern windows, and laying elongated lavender shadows westward on the dewy earth. Through the town dust a June breeze blew, soft and fresh with the odor of growing grass and leaves, spiced by sagebrush and perfumed by fruit blossoms.

It was a good morning to be alive, Dan Ruylander thought, and it was going to be a great relief to get rid of this money he had carried all the way from Cheyenne. Silk Coniff and his fellow thieves were out of luck now, unless they charged the bank. But even if the Rafter funds were safe, Dan's life was not.

The brick bank building stood between Kartmell's Carriage Works at the left and the Draeger Lumber and Coal Yard on the right, as Dan and Terrell approached. The freight traffic had ebbed, and there were few people on the street as yet. Storekeepers swept their porches, and swampers sluiced out the saloons. Somewhere in the distance roosters crowed, cows bawled, and dogs set up a barking.

They had reached the duckboards near the bank, when hoarse angered voices and the smack of knuckles on flesh brought them whirling about. Back in front of the Powder Horn, Kid Antrim had Chill Cahoon draped over a hitch-rail, and Rusty Fergus was slugging it out with Vern Winslett. Then the others piled into it, and identities were lost in a heaving brawling mass of humanity. A gaunt lanky man wearing a badge on his black vest moved toward the gang fight, and Garry Terrell said: "Sheriff Sunderlee will break it up."

Dan Ruylander cursed and started back across, surprised to see old Jud Crater circling away from the scene of the battle toward the lumber and coal yard. Dan wondered what Jud could have spotted to draw him in that direction and leave Rafter outnumbered behind him. Terrell gripped Dan's arm and said: "The sheriff'll stop that, Dan." Then from the dim passage between the carriage shop and the bank issued the familiar mocking voice of Silk Coniff: "Step in here, friend Dan—and you too, mister! Don't reach or you're dead!''

Wheeling around Dan saw Coniff smiling over a gun barrel in the deep purple shadows of the alley. There was nothing to do but obey or get shot down in their tracks. The fight across the street had been most opportune for Silk. As they walked into the alleyway, Dan caught a fleeting glimpse of the lank beak-nosed Tip Haydock covering them from underneath the dark overhang of Kartmell's Carriage Works.

''What is this anyway?'' Garry Terrell asked, in perplexity.

''Holdup,'' Dan Ruylander said wryly. ''Old friends from back home.''

''Crazy,'' muttered Terrell. ''They'll never get out of here, Dan.''

Silk Coniff laughed, backing deeper into the passage and beckoning them on with his pistol. ''We've been in and out of tighter spots than this, Oregon. Shell out, friend Dan. You must be sick of toting that sixty-odd thousand all over the country. We need it more than this bank does, Danny. Let's see the color of it!''

They were hidden from the street now. Glancing over his shoulder, Dan saw Haydock slouching into the alley mouth behind them, and he knew that Bull Klagstad must be out back with the horses. The trap was tight. What few people were on the street would be drawn to the ruckus in front of the Powder Horn. In a rash moment of flaring red rage, Dan Ruylander was tempted to go for his gun, but sanity returned in time to indicate the suicidal folly of such a move. Guns on them, front and rear, and Coniff and Haydock would rather shoot him than not. The sonsabitches had set and sprung the trap.

''You'll never live to spend it, Silk,'' said Dan quietly, stalling for time, banking on their single chance: old Jud Crater.

''That's my problem, not yours,'' Coniff said, the

bright insolence of his eyes matching the curve of his lips. "Dish out, Danny. And make it fast before I get nervous and burn you down."

"You intend to do that anyway, don't you, Silk?"

Coniff laughed. "Why not? You been top dog all your life. I want to see you gutshot and dying in the dirt. Get that money out!"

Dan Ruylander reached left-handed for the thick sheaf of bills in his inside breast pocket. At that instant from behind Dan, the crisp command of Jud Crater brought Tip Haydock spinning about to face the street. Just in time to meet the roaring blast of old Jud's .44. Haydock jerked and doubled over, his pistol exploding into the ground, and then Tip pitched slowly forward and lay stretched full length, with his beaked hawk-face buried in the soil and rubble.

Silk Coniff's sleek head swiveled toward the mouth of the alley, his barrel swerving slightly with his eyes. Dan Ruylander strode in and struck him alongside of the jaw with a right-hand smash, snapping that glossy head and flinging Coniff back against the clapboard wall of the carriage shop with a jarring crash.

Sagging, stunned and drooling blood, Coniff swung his gun to bear on Dan . . . . But Garry Terrell drew with smooth speed and thumbed off a shot before Silk could trigger. The concussion beat thunderously from wall to wall, and Silk Coniff stiffened high against the wood, wagging his head in surprise and protest. His knees gave way, dropping him slackly. Coniff rolled over once and sprawled moaning and helpless on his back at Dan's feet.

Acting on pure instinct, half-dazed from the nearness of death, Dan Ruylander lifted his own Colt from the leather and lined it toward the backyard, just as the massive bulk of Bull Klagstad blotted out the sunlight at the rear of the alley. The Bull had a bead on Terrell, but Dan let go a split-second ahead of him and saw the dust spurt from Klagstad's middle as the slug drilled home. Bull's shot shattered a side window in Kartmell's, as he hunched backward and fell into an awkward sitting position in a litter of rubbish and manure.

Bull Klugstad with trying frenziedly to lift his weapon with both hands, when Dan Ruylander's gun leaped with another flaming blast. The bullet smashed into Bull's chest and threw him flat on his enormous shoulders, legs twitching in the dirt. His head rested at the bottom of a splintered rain barrel, from which a thin stream of water spouted over Klugstad's brutal dying face. Dan watched with his Colt ready, until there was no further movement in that riddled hulk.

The other two were still alive, but Tip Haydock didn't have long. Mumbling incoherently Tip was crawling feebly toward the street, with Jud Crater watching and holding a gun on him. "Told Silk—we'd get it," panted Haydock. "No good—no matter—dead now."

"You had this coming a long time, Tip," said old Jud, not unkindly.

"Maybe so," moaned Tip Haydock, spewing blood and gravel. "No goddamn difference. Man like me—nothing to lose—no way to win." He shuddered, drew up his bony knees, kicked out spasmodically, and was as dead as Klugstad.

Silk Coniff was striving to sit up and talk. "Damn fool play—I pulled. Made you drop belts—we'd had you cold. Lucky, friend Dan. Always lucky." He dropped back and lost consciousness. Jud Crater examined the wound and said: "Silk ain't going to die, I reckon. Better all around if he did, but that one ain't going to kill him. Bastards like that live forever."

At the alley mouth they met Sheriff Sunderlee, with the Rafter and Triangle riders at his heels and a curious crowd gathering behind them. Garry Terrell recited the story to the sheriff, and Sunderlee sent one of his deputies after the doctor for Silk Coniff.

Dan Ruylander spoke to his crew: "No more trouble with Triangle, boys. I mean it, Kid and Rusty . . . . Garry Terrell just saved my life in there."

"And Dan Ruylander saved mine right afterward," Terrell told his men. "And Jud Crater saved the both of us."

"That's right," Dan agreed. "Old Jud sprung us out of that one."

"Hell, my chore was easy enough," Jud Crater said, with a splash of tobacco juice. "Saw the Bull out back and started around after him. Then I noticed Tip sneaking in from this front end, so I switched to him. Haydock was as good as dead when he turned around, but I couldn't get a shot at Silk or the Bull."

The doctor came and had Coniff carried to his office, and Sunderlee's deputies dragged the bodies of Haydock and Klugstad off toward the undertaker's establishment. Their animosity dissolved in the face of graver life-and-death matters, Rafter and Triangle drifted away in two separate groups to discuss the gun battle. Dan Ruylander and Garry Terrell entered the bank, and Jud Crater sat down on the steps and fashioned a cigarette. An excited crowd was trailing the dead men to the undertaker's, and Jud observed this with gentle irony, remembering other gun fights in other far flung frontier settlements.

Dan and Garry were both quick and smooth and sure, plenty good with the six gun, and Jud hated to think of them drawing on each other. But it would come to that eventually, beyond any doubt. It was in the book that way, Jud feared. And a man couldn't get away from whatever fate had written down for him in the book.

Sue Terrell came running across the thoroughfare, wide-eyed and anxious, and Jud Crater stood up and said: "In the bank, ma'am. They're all right, the both of 'em." She thanked him and went into the brick building after her brother and Dan.

Sadie McLain crossed from the hotel, and Jud regarded her coldly. "You'd better beat it, gal. Klugstad and Haydock are dead, and Coniff's going to jail—if he lives."

"Is—is Dan all right, Pop?" she asked shakily.

"No thanks to you, sister—he is. It backfired on your friends this morning."

Sadie's green eyes flashed. "What do you mean, no thanks to me? I didn't have anything to do with this."

"Not much," Jud drawled, with sarcasm. "Didn't Dan tell you he was meeting Terrell today? Maybe he mentioned going to the bank, too. You set him up right pretty, but it didn't quite come off . . . . Get out now, gal, before I turn you over to the law."

"You've got nothing on me, old man."

"You're an accomplice," Jud Crater said. "And you're a—Well, let's call it a professional, to keep it polite. Dust along now, and stay the hell away from Dan Ruylander."

Sadie McLain spread her palms helplessly and turned back the way she had come, walking with her rusty auburn head bent and her shoulders trembling and drooping.

In the bank Dan Ruylander met the president, Mason Werle, and deposited $60,000 in a checking account, vastly relieved to exchange all that currency for a check book. "This almost didn't get here," Dan said. "Those three gunmen have been after it all the way from Wyoming."

"Heard the shooting, Mr. Ruylander," said the banker. "It will be a happy day if this country ever becomes civilized. Now if I can be of any further service to you, don't hesitate to contact me. Garry Terrell is one of our most esteemed clients and citizens, and it's a privilege and pleasure to serve any friend of his."

Dan expressed his gratitude and turned to where Garry was consoling and comforting his sister Sue.

Loitering to twist up and light a cigarette, Dan heard them talking once more about making the drive to Wyoming Territory. That would really fix things. Dan didn't see how he could doublecross Garry Terrell anyway, after what had happened out there in the alley. And after Sue Terrell had looked at him with that promise of intimacy in the future.

Dan Ruylander was sorely troubled in his mind, as the Terrells turned to welcome him with gracious friendly warmth. The tentative plan was to establish himself here, and gain the full confidence of Garry Terrell and the bank. Then to withdraw his funds and pay Triangle with a worthless check, shortly before putting the herd on the road homeward.

But if Garry and Sue persisted in riding east with them, along with a supplementary crew from Triangle, Dan didn't know how in the world he was going to cope with that situation. There did not seem to be any way at all, this side of murder. And wholesale murder, at that.

Eleven

Triangle T, on a broad bench overlooking the beautiful valley of North Powder River twenty miles northwest of Baker City, was about the finest layout Dan Ruylander and the Rafter hands had ever looked upon. Even old Jud Crater was impressed. It made most of the ranches they had seen in Wyoming and Idaho seem crude and primitive in comparison. The home spread of Rafter could not stack up with this outfit, as much as Dan hated to admit it.

The great stone ranch house, the large barns and bunkhouse, the stout corrals, sheds and outbuildings, all had the austere dignity of age embellished with modern improvements and scrupulous caretaking. Triangle had been here longer than most layouts, and from all appearances it would endure forever. It was solid and permanent, as well as gracious and homelike. The grounds and equipment were well-kept, and everyone who worked for this brand took a deep pride in it, from Hawk Fallon down to the lowliest house servant.

Tall Oregon myrtle trees, with fragrant evergreen leaves and clusters of green-gold flowers, shaded the yard. Underneath them grew ornamental grape shrubs with bright amber blossoms, and short white-blooming tea trees. In the background were stands of Douglas fir and spruce, western cedar and hemlock, and the slopes of the foothills and the Blue Mountains to the west were somber and scented with ponderosa pine.

The Rafter crew enjoyed the hospitality of the Terrells for several days, while Dan Ruylander and Jud Crater were buying horses, gear and provisions. They picked the horses from the Triangle herds, big rawboned surefooted geldings of claybank ancestry. Fifty of them in all, three or four years old and weighing twelve hundred or better, fast and strong with splendid lung-power and stamina. Dan bought a powerful mottled gray for himself, and Jud selected a wiry blue roan.

Some of these broncs had to be gentled and trained, and Kid Antrim and Rusty Fergus, the bronc-peeling experts of Rafter, went into action in the breaking pens. Vern Winslett and Chill Cahoon, the foremost twisters for Triangle, contributed their share to this process. The rivalry between the two factions was intense around the corrals, but didn't quite flare into open hostility.

At Kartmell's in Baker City, Dan purchased a Moline chuck wagon with a hinged tailgate, and a large Schuttler for a wood-and-bed wagon. He paid for them with checks drawn on the Land and Cattle Bank next door. Garry Terrell hadn't taken payment for the horses as yet, telling Dan to let it go until the cattle were gathered. Triangle was selling the beef at $15 a head, or $45,000 for a herd of 3,000, which would be worth at least $60,000 on the Wyoming market.

While in town they learned that Silk Coniff was making a good recovery, under arrest and slated to stand trial as soon as he was able. Dan Ruylander wanted to slip away and see Sadie McLain for a few minutes, but old Jud Crater didn't give him the chance.

"She's no goddamn good, boy," Jud declared, with scathing contempt. "She set you up like a target for the Coniff bunch. She tried to get you killed that morning, and you're still burning for the little bitch tramp."

"You're way off, Jud," protested Dan. "I never told her I was going to meet Garry that day, and I never said a word about the bank. Silk was just playing a hunch, and it almost paid off for him . . ." But Dan didn't get to see Sadie, even at a distance. There wasn't time.

They drove the wagons back to Triangle loaded with grub and supplies, and spent another night at the ranch. In the morning they moved out to establish their own headquarters in a spacious Triangle line camp, which had its own corrals and sheds, breaking pens and branding chutes. They brought the horse herd and wagons, and soon Rafter had established a far western branch in Oregon. All hands pitched in to finish taming and teaching the half-wild mounts, and then the trial herd had to be rounded up.

For several weeks Dan Ruylander was too busy to miss Sadie McLain or yearn for Sue Terrell, or to worry much about any extraneous matters and future problems. The days weren't long enough to accomplish the million and one tasks that had to be done. Triangle riders joined Rafter, and worked as hard as the men from Wyoming did.

"Jud, you ever hear how Owen Terrell died?" Dan inquired one evening, as they unsaddled after a long tough day of gathering stock. "Seems to be kind of a mystery about it."

"Never heard nothing definite, that's a fact," Jud Crater said. "Just that he died sudden, and pretty soon after his wife. Melinda had pneumonia but they don't say what ailed Owen. Nobody seems to want to talk about it."

"Strikes me that way, too," Dan Ruylander said thoughtfully. He had seen the double grave, fenced-in on a hilltop overlooking the river terrace on which Triangle was built. One stone for them both, with the names and dates carved on it, and underneath the words: CAME WEST OVER THE OREGON TRAIL IN 1851 AND FOUNDED THE TRIANGLE T RANCH—FOREVER TOGETHER IN LIFE AND IN DEATH. Owen Terrell had died four months after Melinda, two years ago in the spring of 1879. Had it been caused by grief and heartbreak, or the corrosion from a guilty conscience? If Owen had had any conscience.

They ranged the headwaters country from the river bottoms to high canyons and meadows in the Blue Mountains, rounding up cattle and chousing them into the holding ground in a box canyon near the line camp. Prime red Durhams and white-faced Herefords, fat and sleek from the rich hard-cured grama grass of the region. It wasn't like working vicious unruly longhorns, wild from the *brasada* thickets and sweeping plains of Texas. These cattle were gentler, milder, and lacked that menacing spread of horns. But it was rough grueling work nonetheless. Often they were in the saddle from before dawn until after dark, putting in twelve and fifteen hours a day and wearing out entire strings of horses.

It surprised Dan and his comrades how Garry Terrell and Hawk Fallon and their Triangle crew plunged into the manifold operations, as if it were strictly an Oregon project. Although they toiled and sweated side by side, there was still bad blood between the two outfits. Dan expected a boil-over at almost any moment.

Some of the wilder claybanks required further breaking and disciplining. Rusty Fergus and Kid Antrim took a daily beating in the hot dusty corrals, while Chill Cahoon and Vern Winslett went on snapping them out in nearby pens. The other riders took occasional turns at it, too. Dan Ruylander peeled a few broncs himself, and old Jud Crater made one memorable showing on a bucking black brute. For the home outfit, Terrell and Fallon demonstrated that they could twist cayuses with the best in the trade. Competition was keen in every department, but thus far there had been no outbreak of violence.

Sue Terrell spent a lot of time at the line camp, riding herd, helping the Triangle cook Smitty, and tending to the inevitable injuries. She massaged the pain and stiffness out of Kid Antrim's jammed leg, bandaged Rusty Fergus's sprained wrist, and treated a variety of bruises, cuts and rope-burns. She was quietly capable and efficient, kind and considerate yet firm and reliant. Her friendship with Dan Ruylander, deep and instinctive from the start, seemed to be ripening into something richer as time went on. They spent evenings strolling under the cottonwoods and willows of the riverbank, talking before the fireplace in the great stone ranch house at Triangle, and hiking into the hills when the moon was bright.

Hawk Fallon did not like this. There was naked hatred in his odd yellowish eyes every time they fell upon Dan Ruylander. But the Hawk couldn't very well object, as long as Garry Terrell didn't. And Garry seemed to approve fully of Sue's close relationship with Dan.

One night Sue and Dan sat on a hillside above a

moon-dappled sagebrush flat, and a balmy breeze swept the clean scent of highland pines down to mingle with the spicy odor of sage. In the background coyotes cried mournfully at the stars, and the howling of timber wolves was a weird lovely sound in the vast night. Sue Terrell shivered and pressed nearer to Dan, shoulder and hip warm against his.

"When we first met, Dan," she said, "did you have a feeling we knew one another?"

He nodded gravely, the moonbeams gliding his ruffled bronze head. "I did, Sue. It choked me all up, left me tongue-tied and sweating and miserable."

"It was the strangest thing. As if we'd always known each other. Nothing like that ever happened to me before."

"Not to me either. It was kind of a shock. I felt glad and afraid at the same time."

"So did I. What do you suppose it means? That we were destined to meet and maybe fall in love? I even thought of reincarnation, but I can't quite believe in that."

"I don't know, Sue," he said, a trifle taut and ill at ease. Dan wondered if he should kiss her. Perhaps he could make her love him, take her and then leave her. A fitting revenge on the Terrells. But how could he keep from loving her and wanting to marry her? No, that'd never do. He was ashamed of himself for thinking of it.

"But you act rather aloof, Dan," said Sue Terrell. "As if you're holding back or something. Are you still afraid?"

"No, I'm not afraid. But it's a long way from Oregon to Wyoming."

"I'd go anywhere with the man I love, no matter how much it would hurt to leave Garry and Triangle. I think I've talked Garry into going back to Wyoming with you anyway."

"What about Hawk Fallon?"

"He's a good man—in his way. But not for me, Dan. I guess he's still in love with me—as much as a man like him can be. Once, when I was younger, I was a bit infatuated with him, but I outgrew it. Hawk Fallon's a killer, cruel and ruthless. Garry needs him because Fallon is a good foreman, as well as gunman. But Garry wouldn't allow me to go with him, Danny. Not ever. And Garry likes you as well as any man he's ever known."

"I like him too," Dan Ruylander said. "Hasn't Garry got a girl somewhere around here?"

"He had one," Sue Terrell said. "He could have all kinds of them, of course, but he never got over that one. She wasn't a very nice girl either. Dad gave her some money and sent her away three years ago."

Dan went cold and rigid. "What's her name, Sue?"

"Sadie McLain," she said, her eyes sharpening on him. "Why, what's the matter, Dan?"

"I met her down in Utah, on the trip out. Does Garry know she's in Baker City now?"

"I don't believe so," said Sue. "And I hope he doesn't find out. I'm afraid he'd go back to her, now that Dad's gone. Did you—uh—get mixed up with Sadie, Dan?"

"Not really," he lied, prickly heat on his cheeks and forehead. "Just talked with her some. She said there was a man up here, but I never thought of Garry."

"Nobody could understand Garry's interest in her. She used to work in the Silver Barrel in Baker. Probably back there by now. If she is, I suppose Garry will see her sometime, and it'll start all over again. She's no good, is she, Dan?"

"I—I wouldn't know," Dan Ruylander mumbled. "She was in a place called the Gold Nugget in Ogden, so I reckon she can't be much."

"What makes you act so guilty and worried?"

"Nothing, Sue. I'd hate to have Garry get tangled

up with her again, that's all.''

''He will if he sees her,'' Sue said gloomily. ''She's the only woman he ever wanted. Well, there isn't much anyone can do about it.''

Dan grinned. ''Maybe old Jud could make Garry see the light.''

''Why? Did he make you see it, Dan?''

Dan's grin faded. ''No, but old Jud's pretty good at setting anybody straight on things.''

''He would be,'' Sue agreed. ''Jud Crater's a grand old man.''

''How do you like the other Wyoming boys?''

''Fine, all of them. Better than our own riders, to be perfectly frank.'' Her smile creased the sculptured cheeks and squinted her eyes, in that entrancing manner. ''But I have a favorite, you know. A big easy half-shy and half-bold boy by the name of Ruylander.''

Dan laughed. ''That no-account horse thief from the Sweetwater?'' They turned toward one another in mutual accord, and their arms went around locking firmly, and their lips met for the first time and held there. It didn't have the fierce animal frenzy of embracing Sadie McLain. It was sweeter and cleaner and far more satisfyng, the kind of kiss that would grow better with time and repetition. Emotions that would last and burn ever brighter and higher, building upon themselves to undreamed of heights.

As they walked back towards camp, boots swishing through dewy grass and sagebrush beneath tough gnarled junipers and cedars, Sue Terrell spoke in a hushed little-girl voice, ''You know something, Danny? I think I'm in love!''

''I'm afraid we both are, Sue,'' said Dan Ruylander solemnly.

''Why do you say afraid?''

''Because it's so big and new. It kinda scares you.''

''Oh, Dan! My darling Dan,'' she sighed, and they

paused to kiss and cling again, under the radiant silver moon and the steel-sparkling stars. Dan Ruylander knew despairingly that he was lost and in love with this girl, who should have been an enemy. He was a renegade and a traitor to his own father, tricked by fate, as helpless as tumbleweed in the wind.

"Will you take me to the dance in Pondosa Saturday night, Dan?" asked Sue Terrell, as they sauntered onward. "Then there's a big ball in Baker the Fourth of July."

"We'll be road-branding the stock and I'll be all in," Dan said. "Don't shine much on the dance floor anyway. But we'll see, Sue."

"Hawk asked me to go with him. He's a wonderful dancer."

"Maybe you'd better go with him then."

"But I don't want to."

"And I don't want you to either," Dan Ruylander said. He hadn't realized that June was nearly gone, and they'd soon be in the month of July. The herd was practically gathered now, but the cattle had to be branded yet. Plenty of work before they hit the long trail eastward, and Dan was increasingly aware of the relentless pressure of time. If you could only stop the clock, make time stand still for a few days, and lie back and relax and rest without heed of waste. But nobody could do that.

The only way to escape time was to get good and drunk, go on a high lonesome, as the old-timers said in the Southwest. And that was no solution either, for when a man sobered up he had to sweat and strain all the harder to make up for the time he had lost. Time wasted was gone forever, water over the dam. There was no freedom or relief from the pressure of time in day-to-day living. A man never got away from it until he died.

In camp everyone seemed to be sleeping, some within the shack and others rolled up in blankets on the ground, except for the nighthawks on duty out by the canyon entrance. Sue said good night and went into the cabin to find her bed beside Garry's, and Dan sat down on a log by the campfire embers to smoke a final cigarette.

Hearing the crunch of boots behind him, Dan glanced around and saw the tall form of Hawk Fallon striding at him. "Where the hell you been with that girl until this hour?" demanded the Hawk, yellow eyes aflame and mouth thinned tightly. "Speak up, goddamn you!"

Dan Ruylander stood up to face him, watching those strange eagle eyes. "I don't figure that's any of your business, Fallon." This showdown was coming sooner than he'd expected. Dan hoped his Colt .44 was loose in the tied-down holster. He'd need every break possible, if he was to match draws with this gunsharp.

"I'm making it my business, mister," said Hawk Fallon, ice-cold and supremely sure of himself. "I'm going to kill you, Wyoming."

Twelve

Hawk Fallon struck for Dan's face instead of drawing. Struck with lightning ferocity, as though this were too personal an issue to be settled with any weapons other than bare hands. Dan pulled away and rolled with the punch, but even so it jolted his head back and set off a blinding white flash behind his eyeballs. Jarred as he was, Dan Ruylander lashed back instantly, and felt the solid impacts ripple through his hands and arms as Fallon's head rocked and swayed.

They were both bleeding from the first exchange, which might have felled men less superbly conditioned.

Circling, feinting, stabbing and slugging, they fought in grim silence, aware and respectful of each other's power and speed. Their work-toughened hands were bone-hard, bruising and tearing skin wherever they landed. Their muscles were flowing and flexible backed by steel-spring strength, and their big rangy frames were lean and limber as whipcords. None of the sleepers had awakened as yet, and Sue couldn't have heard them inside the log hut.

They fought evenly back and forth, inflicting punishment with unleashed hatred and savage joy. Fallon was a shade stronger, and Ruylander a trifle quicker. Dan could tell when the Hawk was going to throw one by now, and he was beating Fallon to the punch with perfect timing and precision. The Triangle foreman was driven backward, as Dan went on smashing him with solid force. Blood spattered with every blow, and Fallon's head bobbed and twisted under Ruylander's ripping fists. The Hawk tried to hang on and tie up those murderous hands, but Dan belted him loose and kept slashing away.

Fallon's face was a shiny crimson mask in the moonlight, and Ruylander's own features felt numb and enormously swollen. Dan's head was ringing and the metallic taste of blood filled his mouth. His arms were getting heavy, his hands felt broken, and every panting breath seared his tortured lungs. Around the perimeter of camp men were beginning to stir and grumble in their blankets.

Dan Ruylander kept pouring it on with both hands, but Hawk Fallon refused to go down. Then Dan missed and was wide open, and Fallon hit him with a terrific clout on the jaw. Dan's skull seemed to burst on his sprung neck, and he went reeling back on his heels. Fallon closed in clubbing at the head and face, and Dan could not regain his balance, as the earth dipped and tilted under his feet. Something tripped Ruylander as the Hawk lunged in with an elbow gouging at Dan's throat and prying his chin. Dan lurched and fell backward across the log at the fireside, and Fallon landed on top of him with full grinding weight. Agony tore him and Dan thought sure his spine had snapped.

Bearing down brutally, kneeing at Dan's crotch and clawing at his eyes, Hawk Fallon strained mightily to force that tawny head into the red-hot embers of the campfire. Ruylander could feel the scorching heat on his hair and ears, and the log iron-hard beneath his arched aching back. Pain knifed through his groin as Fallon thrust a knee home with crippling power. Dan had to break out of this and soon, or the Hawk would kill him without using a weapon.

Summoning every last atom of strength of will, Dan Ruylander exploded with sudden thrashing fury, bucking and heaving and kicking Fallon off in a tremendous effort born of utter desperation. They fell rolling and sprawling apart on opposite sides of the log, and Dan felt the live coals of the fire through his boots as he scrambled upright. The Hawk was just coming upright when Dan hurdled the dead trunk and hooked him left and right with all he had. Fallon grunted and jerked back, skidding on his shoulder blades ten feet away, the dust rolling up around his long body.

It was then that Sue Terrell screamed from the cabin doorway, and men were up and swarming around but they did not interfere. Dan waited and Fallon got up slowly, the blood flying as he shook off his head. The Hawk had thought Dan was finished, and now Dan had him halfway out, groggy and dazed and sick. The Hawk couldn't believe it. He tried to raise his hands, and was barely able to get them up.

Dan Ruylander went in like a tiger to the kill, both fists flashing as he battered Fallon across the yard and up against the side of the chuck wagon. The Hawk bounced off, head drooping and arms dangling. Dan straightened him with a lashing left, and crossed his right with everything from the heels up behind the punch. It struck with a sodden smash that all but tore Fallon's head off his shoulders.

Hawk slammed into the wagon body, spun and slid along its side, and fell floundering against the huge front wheel. Squirming about and clawing at the spokes, he hauled himself up and whirled about, back against the wheel and right hand dragging at his gun. Dan Ruylander reached for his Colt, but the sheath was empty. Hawk Fallon was clearing and lining his pistol on Dan, and the men that surrounded them were evidently unarmed. Death was close enough to smell and taste.

Sue shouted in wild protest, and then Garry Terrell's clear voice rang out: "Hold it, Fallon! I've got a gun on you and I'll use it. Put that iron down, Hawk!" The Triangle owner paced forward with his gun held steadily on the Hawk, and Fallon spat a mouthful of blood and rammed his weapon back into the holster, mumbling curses.

"I told you I didn't want any fighting here, Hawk," said Terrell.

"You want him keeping your sister out in the hills all night?" Fallon asked, thick-tongued and sobbing for air.

"I'll take care of my sister without your help, Hawk."

"Goddamnit, Garry, I was just looking out for the family."

"Maybe you meant well, but you were wrong, Hawk," said Garry Terrell. "Dan, I'm sorry this had to happen."

'It's all right, Garry," said Ruylander, searching the ground for his gun. Big Barnhorst handed it to him, whispering, "Nice work, Danny. You did a good job on him."

Terrell spoke again: "The next Triangle man that starts trouble is all through. I don't care a damn who it is. That goes for you, Hawk, as well as the rest of the boys."

"I can pull out right now, if you want," Fallon said sullenly, blowing blood and sand from his pulped scarlet lips. His eyes were gashed and swollen nearly shut, and his nose looked flat and broken.

"You can if you like," said Terrell. "But it wouldn't be very smart to leave Triangle and a job like yours."

Still leaning on the wagon wheel, Hawk Fallon glowered at the ground. "All right, Garry, forget it," he said finally. "The hell with it. But I'll settle with Ruylander before I'm done. On my own time and in my own way."

"Any time you want it, Fallon," drawled Dan. "I'll be glad to oblige you." He walked to the horse trough, soaking his raw sore hand and then ducking his throbbing head and washing his blood-smeared face. The cold water was soothing and refreshing, and Dan felt better when he straightened up dripping.

Sue Terrell stood there watching him with anxiety. "Are you really all right, Dan? Come in the cabin and let me look at your face."

"My hands hurt more than my face, Sue," said Dan Ruylander, with a crooked painful grin. "I'm all right. No real damage."

"You'll have to watch Fallon," she said. "Nobody ever whipped him before, Dan. He'll live just to get even with you."

Old Jud Crater drifted by, saying: "Use a gun next time, son. It's easier and quicker and a lot more final."

Garry Terrell came over and asked. "You hurt bad, Dan? It's a damn shame, but I don't think Hawk will try it again. He's needed a licking for a long time, and you gave him a good one. I doubt if he'll risk his job, but we'll keep an eye on him. Now we'd better get some sleep."

Sue pressed Dan's wet arm and went back into the log house. Garry scanned Dan's welted misshapen face. "You two act different tonight. In love, maybe? Well, it couldn't happen to two nicer people."

That's what you think, boy, mused Dan Ruylander ruefully. *If you only knew, Garry. If you only knew what a mucked-up mess this really is.*

"There's an empty bunk inside if you want it, Dan," said Terrell.

"Thanks, Garry. But I like it out here."

"Good night, then." Terrell entered the lamplit cabin, and Sue came out with some ointment, which she rubbed gently into Ruylander's burning face and knuckles.

Triangle had bedded down again on its side of the yard, with Pike Urbom and Otis Sowerby working over the mutilated Fallon.

Dan thanked Sue and she blew him a kiss and went back inside. Hauling his bedroll out of the Schuttler wagon, Dan carried it to the Rafter bivouac. The boys were smoking cigarettes, discussing the fight, and waiting for Dan Ruylander.

Kiowa Kempter and Barnhorst spread out the blankets for him, while Dan shucked off his brush jacket and boots and gun belt. Kid Antrim and Rusty Fergus were jubilant over the beating Dan had given the great Hawk Fallon. Old Jud Crater was sleeping inside tonight.

Barney had a bottle which he passed around, and finally they settled down in their soogans for the night. The reaction wouldn't let Dan Ruylander sleep at once, although he was weary to the bone. His hands ached into his wrists, and a cramping pain stabbed his abdomen. His neck felt wrenched and disjointed, and dull steady anguish ate at his spinal column. The salve had eased his knuckles and facial abrasions somewhat.

But the night was going to be a rough and endless one, and tomorrow would be a day of agony in furnace heat, smothering dust and scalding saddle leather.

Thirteen

July had come with blazing summer heat, and the combined crews of Rafter and Triangle were road-branding the gathered cattle at the line camp on the North Powder.

It was a busy and hectic time for all hands, and Dan Ruylander often wondered why the Terrells were being so generous and helpful. They maintained another crew at the home ranch, but their tophands were working for Rafter. This only made it the more difficult and distasteful for Dan to contemplate doublecrossing Triangle, as he must eventually—unless he disobeyed his father's instructions. And there was Sue Terrell to complicate matters still further. It was a torturous trying interval for Dan Ruylander. Only the exhausting grind of toil made it endurable.

Sue and Garry practically lived at the line camp now, working as hard as any of the men. A good cowhand in her own right, Sue helped hold the herd, cut out stock, and feed the branding pits. When not in the saddle she was assisting Smitty, the cook, or attending to injured cowboys. She could do all these things and still remain wholly feminine, a fact which Dan marveled at.

"I needed this, Dan," said Garry Terrell. "Best thing that's happened to me for some time. I was beginning to get soft and lazy, and resorting too much to the bottle." He and Hawk Fallon were real cattle men and no mistake, vying with Dan Ruylander and Jud Crater, who seemed to be everywhere at once from the holding ground to the branding fires. Those four riders ranged all over the place working without show or strain or wasted motions, their efforts so simple and natural that they seemed to be taking it easy most of the time.

Holding stock and turning back strays. Cutting out and driving critters into the chutes. There the rope men picked them up, forefooting and heeling and stretching them out for the branding iron. Dan and Jud did most of the cutting, with Antrim and Fergus spinning their expert loops to throw the animals. Big Barnhorst and Kiowa Kempter labored with hot irons in the glaring heat and smoking dust of the Rafter branding pen. Occasionally they swapped off, with Dan and Jud sometimes spelling the ropers and then the iron men.

Triangle worked in a similar pattern to feed their separate branding pit. Terrell and Fallon cutting out beeves, with Cahoon and Winslett throwing the ropes, and Sowerby and Urbom sweating on the irons. They too shifted around to break the monotony, while extra Oregon buckaroos held the herd and wrangled the remuda.

Dan Ruylander's big gray claybank had developed into a fine all-around cow horse, remarkably adept and swift at cutting and turning, sharp and solid when it came to roping. It was a pleasure to work stock on a mount like that, but Dan used him only a limited time each day. It was necessary to switch horse frequently, and a man worked out his entire string during the day. When the work was done and the sun was setting behind the Blue Mountains, most of the riders stripped and plunged into the North Powder to wash off the sweat and grime. And came out hungry enough to eat raw steaks off a live cow critter, as some of the boys put it.

It was a hard life but a good full one, with action enough to satisfy any man who required that element to round out his existence. Even the young hellers like

Rusty Fergus and Kid Antrim.

Dan Ruylander's face had healed well, leaving only a few faint marks on the deeply bronzed skin, but Hawk Fallon would never look quite the same again. The Hawk was scarred for life, his nose bent crooked, and his hate for Dan was an evil tangible thing that made everybody in camp uncomfortable. It was particularly irksome and unpleasant for Dan to feel that unrelenting hatred directed at him every hour of every day. There'd be no peace for Dan, until Hawk Fallon was dead. It was fairly certain by this time, however, that Fallon meant to abide by Terrell's ruling and make no further move against Dan on the job.

"How much am I going to owe you for wages when this is over?" Dan Ruylander asked Terrell one evening, as they dried themselves on the riverbank after a refreshing bath and swim.

"Not a cent, Dan," said Garry. "We're donating the labor."

"But why, Garry? I don't get it."

Terrell laughed and slapped Dan's bare muscular back. "Call it I like you and can afford it, Danny. Wasn't enough work to keep these boys busy on the home spread. Call it a campaign to promote good will between Oregon and Wyoming. Or maybe I'm doing it for a prospective brother-in-law, Dan. But mainly I'm doing it because I want to, which I consider reason enough."

"I don't know, Garry. It doesn't seem right . . . ."

"Forget it, boy," said Garry Terrell. "Now tomorrow's the Fourth, Dan. Sue and I are riding to Triangle tonight. We have to be in Baker for the Independence Day celebration, whether we want to or not. I'm giving our boys the day off. Why don't you declare a holiday and come with us? We've all been slaving too hard here, Dan."

Ruylander thought it over and shook his damp head.

"Guess we'll work tomorrow, Garry. Maybe we can finish branding the last batch of stock. Like to get it over and throw them on the road as soon as possible. It's a two-month drive and we want to get home early in September. Dad'll need us for fall roundup, if we can make it that fast."

"Well, you're the boss, Dan. But you'll come in tomorrow night, won't you?" They were dressing now, with others laughing along the shore.

"Yeah, we'll make the evening festivities. Got to give this outfit a chance to hooraw and howl, before the boys bust wide open."

"I think we'll make the drive with you, Dan—if you want us. Save hunting up and hiring another crew."

"Rafter will pay them regular wages on the road, at least," Dan Ruylander said. "That's got to be understood, Garry."

"Maybe you'd rather not have us along. I know damn well you don't want Fallon."

"Would he have to come?"

"Afraid so, Dan," said Terrell. "Hawk can keep those other four in line better than I or anyone else ever could. I know they aren't easy to handle, but you've got to admit they're damn good hands."

"They're that all right," Dan said slowly. "Well, we'll see when the time comes."

"Watch out for the Hawk in town," Terrell warned. "He might try something, seeing he's off duty and away from the ranch."

"I ought to call him and get it over with," said Dan Ruylander glumly. "It's getting on my nerves pretty bad, Garry. I've got enough troubles without that always on my back."

"I know, it's a tough spot for you, Dan," said Terrell, with sympathy. "I'd fire Fallon in a minute, if he wasn't the best foreman in eastern Oregon."

Dan smiled somberly. "You wouldn't want me to kill

him then?''

"No, I wouldn't," Terrell said honestly. "But I'd rather have that happen, Dan, than to have the Hawk kill you."

Ruylander wondered if he actually meant that. Garry sounded sincere, but after all he was Owen Terrell's son. And Sue was Owen's daughter. How far could you trust either one of them, behind the charming surface they showed to the world? Dan didn't know. He liked Garry and he loved Sue, yet he remained dubious about them. They might even know the story of Dirk Ruylander, and be playing a deeper and more intricate game that anyone imagined.

That evening the Wyoming men had the camp to themselves, and it was a relief to have Hawk Fallon and his four henchmen gone. The Terrells and most of the Triangle crew had pulled out for home and the Fourth of July festival in Baker City, leaving behind two horse wranglers and four night-riders to patrol the bed ground of the herd. Garry had done this so Rafter could get a full night's rest. He couldn't have been more considerate, if Dan had been a blood brother.

"They want to make the drive with us, Jud, and bring along their crew," Dan Ruylander said, as they lounged at ease about the campfire.

"Well, if we have 'em with us, Dan," said Jud Crater, "we won't have to be watching the back-trail or fighting 'em off all the way home."

"We'll be fighting them just the same though," Dan murmured.

"That's for sure," agreed big Barnhorst. "There's Fallon sworn to get Dan, and Pike Urbom hates my guts. Sowerby can't hardly wait to get a crack at the Injun here. And sparks fly plenty every time Cahoon and Winslett come anywhere near the Kid and the Redhead."

"Leaves me to referee," Jud Crater drawled. "Or

throw down on Garry and the gal."

"Why they treating us so good, doing so much for us?" asked Kiowa Kempter. "Maybe fatting us up for the kill?"

"I think Garry and Sue are on the level," Kid Antrim said. "Real quality folks, them two. But that bunch of bastards they got riding for 'em turns my stomach inside out."

"Yeah, the Terrells themselves are ace-high," said Rusty Fergus. "But I can't stand them lowdown lizards they hire. My knuckles and my trigger-finger are itching day and night."

Dan Ruylander puffed slowly on his pipe. "But how we going to handle 'em, boys?"

"We can handle 'em easier in Wyoming than out here, Danny," said old Jud, munching on his chew.

"But we can't just kill 'em all, Jud."

"All but the Terrells would suit me fine," Barnhorst said, a grin wrinkling his rugged face. "Then you can marry Sue, Danny, and send Garry back to Oregon."

Dan stared into the low-burning fire. "You think Garry'll hold still for that, Barney?"

"He seems to like you plenty, Dan."

"Yeah, he seems to . . ."

Kid Antrim kicked at the turf. "I don't like these undercover games. I like to see the cards and the chips on the table."

"Sometimes, Kid, you have to play dealer's choice," Jud Crater reminded him.

Dan Ruylander sighed and stretched his long limbs. "It's a hell of a situation, any way you look at it. I reckon we'll just have to take things as they come."

"There ain't no other way that I can see, son," said Jud Crater.

Kid Antrim cocked his tow head. "Cheer up, men. Tomorrow night we'll be in Baker City. Long time since we had any fun."

"You ain't going hog wild, just because it's the Fourth," warned Jud. "If there's any fireworks let the natives furnish 'em. We're a long ways from home, Kid."

"What an outfit!" grumbled Rusty Fergus, shaking his fiery head in mock disgust. "A slave-driving boss like Dan and a psalm-singing old mountain preacher like Jud to spoil everything. If I'd a known I'd a jumped off that train way back in Rawlins and hit home to Rafter."

"Sometimes I wish you and the Kid had both done that," Jud Crater said acidly.

Kid Antrim laughed jeeringly. "You'd have been in great shape without me and the Redhead. Not a one of you that can twist a bronc or sling a rope! You oughta thank God you got us, Jud."

Crater spat a sizzling charge into the glowing embers. "I thank God we ain't got any more like you, and that's a fact."

Dan Ruylander, laughing with the rest, said, "Better bed down, boys. Tough day tomorrow."

"Imagine working like dogs on Independence Day?" groaned Rusty Fergus. "It ain't even patriotic. There oughta be a law against it."

As Dan settled into his bedroll, the Kid and Rusty were crooning in a sorrowful harmony:

> *"I ain't got no use for the wimmen,*
> *A true one ain't never been found,*
> *They use a man for his money,*
> *When it's gone they turn him down . . . .*
>
> *They're all alike at the bottom,*
> *Selfish and grasping for all,*
> *They stick by your side when you're winning,*
> *And laugh in your teeth at your fall."*

Fourteen

Baker City, hung with flags and draped in red-white-and-blue bunting, wore a carnival air of gay hilarity when Rafter rode in the night of the Fourth. The tie-racks were lined with saddle broncs, buggies, buckboards and wagons, and the board walks were thronged with pedestrians in various stages of inebriety. Drunken riders raced through the streets, whooping and firing pistols into the air, as people scattered before them. Music blared from crowded saloons and dance halls, punctuated by gunshots and bursting firecrackers. Rockets and Roman candles soared high overhead, tracing the night sky with fiery colorful streamers.

The men from Wyoming left their horses at the livery barn, and stretched saddle-racked limbs and bodies. They had knocked off early, the branding not quite completed, because Dan Ruylander knew the boys were eager to get into town. They had shaved, bathed in the river, dressed in clean clothing, and started for Baker, a thirty-mile ride from the line camp. They should have been ready for bed instead of a celebration, but this atmosphere of gaudy merriment was like a tonic after weeks on the open range.

The ball was on in the town hall, and Dan supposed that Sue and Garry Terrell were in attendance there, but he had no inclination for such a formal and proper affair. Dan preferred to hit the saloons and honky-tonks with his comrades tonight, and they began making the rounds at once. There were drunks everywhere and a few brawls broke out now and then, but for the most part a holiday spirit prevailed and the revelers were good-natured and jolly. Dan Ruylander was on the watch for Hawk Fallon, but saw neither him nor the other Triangle gunhands. They were probably dancing at the ball, or seeking earthier pleasures down the line in some parlor house.

When the Rafter crew reached the Silver Barrel, Dan looked around for Sadie McLain. The place swarmed with painted women in bright low-cut gowns, but Sadie was not among them. Rusty Fergus and Kid Antrim found partners and took the dance floor, while Big Barnhorst and Kiowa Kempter tried their luck at the faro layout. After a few more drinks at the bar with Jud Crater, Dan said:

"The boys seem to like it here. I'm going to wander around a little. Keep an eye on them, Jud."

Crater snorted. "Hunting for that sorrel filly, I reckon. Well, if you don't know no better, go on and be goddamned, for all I care."

"I'm not heavy with money any more, Jud."

"There's things to worry about besides money."

"I won't get into any trouble," Dan promised. "So long, Jud."

The little veteran turned back to the bar without responding, and Dan walked out through milling groups of men and women, and the heady fumes of whiskey, perfume and perspiration. On the slat walk a voice called, "Hey, Ruylander," and Dan wheeled with his hand on the lowslung .44. But it was the lank cadaverous Sheriff Sunderlee, looking more melancholy and bored than ever.

"You ought to know that sonofabitch Silk Coniff broke out and got away," Sunderlee said, deep-toned and sorrowful. "Them deputies of mine ain't worth a goddamn. Don't think Coniff's still hereabouts, but he might be. If he is he'll be gunning for you again, so keep your eyes peeled. He sure wants you dead, son."

"Thanks, Sheriff," said Dan. "I'll be on the lookout

for him. I was hoping you'd put him away for a while."

"Too bad you boys didn't kill him that morning by the bank," Sunderlee said. "It takes bullets to stop a renegade like Coniff. Jails ain't worth a damn for his kind."

"Well, you had him under arrest, at least. That's more'n they ever did back in Wyoming."

"Got a hunch he lit a shuck back that way, but I don't know for sure. Could be hid out around here. There's enough ratholes for him. Be ready anyway, boy."

"I will," Dan said. "And thanks again, Sheriff."

So there are two of them again, who want to shoot me. Hawk Fallon and Silk Coniff. This gets better all the time, Dan Ruylander mused, drifting along through jostling hordes of merrymakers in the direction of the Great Northwest House. He wanted to see if Sadie was still there. Just to talk with her. She might know what had become of Silk Coniff. She wasn't apt to be in her room on this gala night, but he'd try it anyway. Dan doubted that Sadie had seen Garry Terrell, but they might have got together this evening.

Dan Ruylander entered the hotel and climbed the stairs. The door that had been Sadie's was outlined in light. The room might be occupied by someone else now, but he was willing to take a chance. His heart quickened and his throat swelled full, as he knocked on the panel. This was one hotel room that Dan would never forget.

The door opened narrowly and the coppery-red head and sharp features of Sadie McLain appeared in the aperture. "If it isn't Mr. Ruylander! To what do I owe this great honor?"

"Are you alone, Sadie?"

"You think I've got a roomful of customers? What do you want?" She was cryptic and bitter.

"I want to talk to you," Dan said evenly.

"I'm flattered, I'm sure. But you're risking your reputation, Mr. Ruylander. What do you want to talk about?"

"Lots of things." He pushed gently but firmly on the door.

Sadie McLain yielded with a scornful laugh. "Don't forget to draw your gun."

"Thanks for reminding me." Dan flipped the Colt clear of the sheath and stepped inside. The room was as empty as it had been that first night. A bottle of brandy stood on the table as before, beside a pile of newspapers, magazines and *Godey's Lady's Book.* "Funny way to spend the Fourth, Sadie,' he said, holstering the gun.

"Just another day to me."

"What's wrong with you anyway?"

Her laugh was harsh. "You expect to me to greet you with open arms?"

"Not hardly but—"

"I suppose you think I was working with Coniff all the time?"

"No, I don't, Sadie."

"What kept you away for a whole month then?"

"I've been busy," Dan Ruylander said. "Gathering a herd up on the North Powder. Only been to town once, and that was to buy wagons and provisions. I haven't seen anything but cowboys on horses and cows."

Sadie smiled with malice. "And Sue Terrell. Well, I'll offer you a drink, Dan. But that's all you'll get."

"All I want."

She laughed mockingly. "I should think so, after a month with that rich cowgirl of yours! But I don't blame you, Wyoming. I haven't got a ranch and a bankful of money. You're a smart boy, Danny."

"Cut it out, Sadie." He accepted the glass of brandy and slouched wearily on the edge of the bed, while Sadie seated herself in what passed for an easy chair in the

Great Northwest. "Have you seen Silk Coniff since he busted out?"

"No, I haven't," she answered promptly. "But I saw a lot of law for a few days. Your godfather must've tipped them off, I guess. They thought sure Silk would try to see me, but he was too smart for them. When you leaving for Wyoming, Dan?"

"In about a week, I expect."

"I hear the Terrells are going with you."

"Has Garry been here?"

"So you know about that too?" Sadie McLain said. "No, I haven't seen Garry—yet. But I will. Maybe he'll take me along on the trail drive. Wouldn't that be lovely, Dan? Two handsome young couples of us."

"Why don't you leave Garry alone, Sadie?"

"Why don't you go to hell?" she said viciously. "And start right now before I give you this glass in the face, Mr. Ruylander!"

Dan smiled at her. "Red hair and green eyes. I always heard that was a deadly combination."

"You have no idea how deadly. Go on, get out of here!"

"You're always telling me to get out."

"This time I mean it, and this time you're going, brother." Sadie was cold and hard as steel, with a wicked glitter in her green eyes.

Dan Ruylander drained his glass and rose tall and limber. "Sure, Sadie, I'll go. Sorry you feel this way."

"How should a girl feel? Beat it, you big bastard!"

Putting on his hat with a thin smile Dan walked to the door. So this was the way it ended—sometimes. He did not care much. Her perfume seemed unpleasant tonight, smelling as old Jud had described it, and her brazen hardness was straight from the brothel. You couldn't reach or touch women like that. They weren't quite human, and a man was absolutely helpless with them. Dan felt sorry for Garry Terrell.

109

Stepping outside Dan sensed another presence on the stairway, as he turned to close the door after himself. Sadie called, "Don't come back either!" And he said: "That'll be easy."

Dan Ruylander started for the head of the stairs, and halted with a chilling shock of surprise. Garry Terrell was standing there, tall and immaculate, staring at Dan with naked venom. The change in that handsome face was appalling. Garry looked now as Owen Terrell must have looked that night over the card table in the sutler's loft at Fort Laramie, three decades ago. Stripped of charm and polish, the evil and fury and hatred shining through. And Dan thought: *Here is my true enemy. Not Hawk Fallon or Silk Coniff. This is the man to be reckoned with and feared, just as Dad warned me . . . . Garry, the son of Owen Terrell.*

"So my sister isn't woman enough for you?" Garry said, his voice as different as his features. "You have to play the field. What kind of wild stallions do they raise in Wyoming?"

"I met this girl in Utah," said Dan Ruylander. "We were only talking."

Terrell laughed without humor or sound. "Don't feed me that, fella. Sadie's no conversationalist. I like the way you repay our hospitality, Ruylander. It seems that Fallon was right about you. I should have let him shoot you."

"I tell you this was perfectly innocent, Garry."

"Nothing is innocent with Sadie McLain. I ought to know; it's put me through hell. But *you,* coming from my sister to *her!* That's too much. Too goddamn much altogether!"

"Won't you listen to reason at all?"

"You can't crawl out of this one," Garry Terrell said, lips thinned and baring his white teeth.

"I'm not trying to crawl out of anything."

"You rotten lecher! You want every woman you

110

meet, whether they're good or bad? You go from one to another like a rutting bull, Ruylander. From my own sister to the girl I wanted to marry three years ago.''

"You're either crazy or drunk, man," said Dan. "Get hold of yourself and cool down a little. I won't take much more from you."

"Why, you sonofabitch!" Terrell snarled.

"You've gone too far," Dan said. "How do you want it? Guns or fists?"

Garry Terrell struck without warning, smashing Dan full in the face and driving his head back. Recovering quickly Dan ducked under the flailing arms and lunged in, ramming a shoulder into Terrell's body and slamming him backward against the far wall. The breath whistled through Terrell's teeth from the crushing impact, but with an explosive burst of strength he heaved Dan off and rushed him across the corridor. Ruylander's head and shoulders crashed into the wall beside Sadie's door with jarring force, and the door opened and then banged shut again.

Crowding close and pinning Dan to the wall, Garry kneed brutally at his abdomen and chopped at the face with both hands. Pain ripped through Ruylander's body and lights flashed in his skull. With a supreme wrenching effort he came off the barrier and hurled Terrell away. The man was staggering off balance, when Dan charged and caught him with whipping lefts and rights. Garry went down and rolled against the baseboard with a heavy thump. Other doors opened along the hallway, but nobody emerged to try to stop the fight.

On hands and knees Garry Terrell swayed there, dark curly head hanging and blood dripping to the frayed carpet. Dan knew he had connected solidly, and thought Terrell might stay down. But he was faking to throw Dan off guard, and suddenly he came driving along the floor like a huge projectile. His shoulder struck Dan's knees, his arms wrapping around the legs, and they fell in a threshing welter at the head of the staircase.

Dan Ruylander, rolling with the momentum of that hurtling tackle, heaved Terrell overhead and somersaulted after him down the steps. Garry grappled onto Dan and they tumbled downstairs together, striking savagely with fists, elbows and knees as they bumped and jolted from one tread to another. Rolling over and over in that furious embrace, they thrashed to a stop near the bottom of the stairway, with Dan sprawled above Terrell and crosswise on the steps.

Shaken and dazed, Dan Ruylander saw Garry rear up on his knees and reach for his gun, with the look of murder on his sweaty crimsoned face. Dan didn't have time to do anything but lash out with his boots. They landed squarely under Terrell's jawbone, and flung him over backward. His gun flew clear and his head struck the floor at the foot of the stairs.

When Dan hooked an arm over the banister and hoisted himself erect, Garry Terrell was stretched in a senseless sprawl on the lobby floor. The desk clerk and other men gathered about, and someone said: "It's that boy from Wyoming and young Terrell, and Garry looks mighty dead. I wouldn't want to be in your boots, Wyoming."

"Just knocked out, that's all," Dan Ruylander panted. "Get some water and towels, and I'll bring him to."

"He'll kill you when he comes to, boy."

"Not tonight," Dan said, limping over to pick up Terrell's gun. "Give me a hand with him, somebody."

They carried the unconscious Terrell to a leather couch. The clerk brought towels and a basin of water, and another man fetched a glass of whiskey from the hotel bar. Dan Ruylander started sponging Garry's face and head, and an onlooker said:

"Ain't that something? He beats and kicks the living

shit out of a man, and then he nurses him like a baby!''

"I don't like to use the boots," Dan said. "But he was reaching for his gun, and I didn't have any choice. It was just a friendly little argument."

"Hate to see you boys get at it when you're riled up then," muttered the clerk. "I was going to call the sheriff, until I saw it was Garry Terrell."

"They don't arrest Terrells in these parts, do they?" asked Dan.

The spectators snickered and one of them said: "Not if they want to stay in office, they don't."

"What kind of a man was Owen Terrell?" inquired Dan.

"Never heard nothing against him," was the cautious response. "He was too big for anybody to run him down. In public anyhow."

Garry Terrell came to with an expression of total bewilderment. Gradually his eyes cleared and focused, and the fanatical fury and hate were gone from them. "You still here, Dan?" he murmured weakly.

"Why not, Garry?" said Ruylander. "Thought you might feel differently when you came out of it. If you don't, I can pull out."

Terrell's head stirred sideways. "No, I was wrong, Dan. Must have gone crazy for a minute."

"I want you to get it straight, Garry," said Dan. "There's nothing between Sadie and me. She knew Silk Coniff. I heard that Silk broke out, and I thought she might know where he was. So I went up to ask her. She claimed she didn't know. That's all there was to it."

"It doesn't matter," Garry Terrell said wearily. "I guess Sue told you about Sadie and myself. She's no good—never was and never will be. But she had something for me, Dan. And I can't seem to get her out of my system."

"Those things happen."

Terrell groaned and touched his raw lumped face.

"Feel like I been through a meat-chopper." He moved his arms and legs experimentally. "Hope you can forgive me, Dan. I was out of my head for sure."

"That's okay, Garry," said Dan Ruylander, rinsing the crusted blood off his own lean sweat-glazed face. "No harm done—except I left most of my hide on those stairs, by the feeling."

"Me, too." Terrell sat up carefully and moaned. "I owe you several dozen drinks, Danny. Let's get to work on them."

"Aren't you going up to see Sadie?"

"Later—maybe," Garry Terrell said slowly. "Right now I need liquor more than anything else. God, but I'm disgusted and ashamed of myself. That's the taste I want to wash out, Dan."

"Come on, then." Dan handed his gun back to him. "Hated to kick you in the jaw, Garry, but you were going for that iron."

Terrell grimaced and shook his wet black curls. "I ought to be horsewhipped, Dan. I lay down the law about fighting, and then break it myself. With a friend like you, over a cheap honky-tonk chippie."

"Let's forget it, boy," said Dan Ruylander. "Is Sue having a good time at the ball?"

"Not very," Terrell said. "She was watching and waiting for you all evening, Dan."

"Maybe I'd better look her up."

"After we split a bottle of the best whiskey in Baker City," said Garry Terrell. "I want to apologize for everything, Danny. And drown the whole damn business deep and dead."

Fifteen

Coming to in what seemed to be a suffocating furnace, Dan Ruylander found himself lying fully dressed and sweat-soaked on a strange bed, with old Jud Crater sprawled like a dead man at his side. Sitting up with laborious effort Dan groaned in remorseful anguish as sunlight splintered through throbbing eyes into the chaotic roar of his head. An evil taste gagged him. His tongue was swollen thick and leathery, foully crusted in his burning dry mouth.

Gradually the events of last night returned to his numb and stricken brain. This was a guest room in the clubhouse of the Powder River Stockmen's Association. He and Garry Terrell, indulging in a drinking bout to erase the unpleasantness of their fight, had never got beyond the club bar. Dan hadn't seen Sue Terrell at all . . . . Sometime late Garry had vanished and Crater had appeared, trying to enlist Dan's aid in routing the other four Rafter hands out of some den of vice where they were carousing. The intentions of Dan and Jud had been good, but the drinks were coming too fast and they never did escape from the clubhouse barroom.

Dan turned with another moan to arouse Jud, but the little man was already raising himself from the bed. He wore such an expression of horror and misery that Dan croaked with dry laughter, in spite of his own torment. Jud Crater limped to the washstand and gulped greedily from a water pitcher, and Ruylander rose on wooden legs to wrest the vessel from Jud's grasp and ease his parched throat.

"Where'd you say the boys were?" asked Dan, as

they pulled on their boots and buckled on their gun belts.

"They was down the line in some fancy house. Most likely they're in jail by now. Danny, I feel as bad as you look."

"You ought to see yourself, Jud. Let's go bail 'em out."

"I ain't a morning drinker as a rule," Jud said, more gravel-voiced than ever. "But I'm going to bust that rule today. It's high noon instead of morning anyway, I reckon."

"I'll join you on this special occasion, Jud," said Dan Ruylander. "It's the only kind of breakfast I can think of without shuddering."

They had a couple of drinks at the bar, and learned that Terrell had not returned to the club. He was probably with Sadie McLain in the Great Northwest House, and Dan didn't know whether that was bad or good. The liquor quieted their nerves, eased the tension, and restored some life and vitality to their systems. They felt a bit better as they left the clubhouse and walked toward the sheriff's office and jail.

Sunderlee raised a solemn sunken-cheeked face from his desk, a wad of snuff under his long upper lip, a look of patient suffering in his gloomy eyes. "They ain't in jail but they sure as hell ought to be. And would be if my deputies wasn't so goddamn gutless and chicken-hearted. They're down the line in Idaho Imogene's joint. Threw out the other customers, won't let nobody else in or out, took over the place complete. They ain't killed nobody—yet."

"Much damage, Sheriff?" inquired Dan Ruylander.

"Enough. Not as much as Imogene'll charge but considerable. The house looks like giant powder was set off in it. Nothing personal, but I ain't going to be sorry when your outfit lights out for Wyoming."

Dan grinned. "Don't know as I blame you, Sheriff.

Well, Jud, we'll have to dig 'em out of there."

"You'll need plenty of money, son," Sunderlee said dryly. "Idaho Imogene's plumb mercenary. You might say greedy."

"I'll pay—within reason."

"There won't be nothing reasonable about Imogene today, Ruylander," said the sheriff, with a sad smile. "I was down there with my deputies, but we could't get 'em out without starting a shooting match. And my men wasn't up to it."

"Let us borrow a couple of badges," Dan suggested. "I'm willing to make a fair settlement but I don't want to get held up too much."

After some pondering Sunderlee produced two deputy's stars. "Just so you settle up fair, son. She'd want the price of that herd, if she knew you was buying one off Triangle. With the badges maybe you can get her down somewhere near sensible."

"Maybe you better come along, Sheriff," said Jud Crater.

Sunderlee shook his head, "I've had enough fun for one Fourth." He smiled with surprising warmth. "If you should run across Silk Coniff bring him in too. Dead or alive, it don't matter. I'll stand behind them badges for you. Like to see that sonofabitch hung."

With the stars pinned on their vests, Dan and Jud walked down the line, a double row of parlor houses extending south of Baker City, all silent at midday except for the one operated by Idaho Imogene. Even without the noise, it would have been simple enough to single out that establishment. Broken windows gaped raggedly and the shattered front door hung askew. Sections of the porch rail had been torn out, and feminine garments fluttered like flags from some of the wrecked windowsills, along with a pair of Levis.

"The other customers must have left against their will," Dan remarked. "And at least one without his

117

pants.''

Jud Crater coughed on his first chew of the day. ''Them wildcats of ours sure raised hell. Rusty and the Kid gunwhipped a few while Barney and the Injun beat up the rest and slung them out the doors and windows. At one time last night human bodies was raining out of that place, Dan. It looked like Dodge at the peak of the boom.''

''I don't suppose you and Dad ever busted up any whorehouses down there, Jud?'' said Dan Ruylander. ''Never tried to tree Dodge or Abilene?''

Crater scowled to cover his grin. ''We had more sense than you young jaybirds. We was gentleman compared to you hellhounds today.''

''Yeah, I can imagine,'' Dan said soberly. ''You and Dirk a pair of meek innocent little lambs in those Kansas trail towns. A wonder you lived through it.''

''We was lucky, I guess,'' Jud Crater drawled, munching his tobacco with more relish. ''Just plain lucky, old Dirk and me.''

Music and laughter sounded from the battered bordello, and the gay clear voices of Kid Antrim and Rusty Fergus were lifted in song:

> *''He was only a lavender cowboy,*
> *And the hairs on his chest were but two;*
> *But he wanted to ride with the he-men,*
> *And fight like the heroes do-oo!''*

Idaho Imogene, a huge corpulent woman of immense dignity, met Dan and Jud at the ruined doorway and glanced suspiciously at their faces and badges. ''You ain't the law. I never saw either one of you before. What you trying to pull of here?''

''The sheriff deputized us to arrest these men, ma'am,'' Dan told her. ''Wouldn't you like to get rid of them?''

''Gawd, yes!'' said Imogene. ''We ain't slept a wink.

118

They've wrecked my whole house, drove off all my best customers, scared my little girls 'most to death, and drunk up all my whiskey. I want to get rid of 'em, but I want the damages paid first. That'll run a thousand dollars, New Deputy.''

"The sheriff said a couple hundred dollars would cover it, ma'am.''

Idaho Imogene screamed, as if in mortal agony. "A coupla hundred? Why, that won't pay for an hour's trade out of all we lost, you fool! What's the matter with that jugheaded Sunderlee? He can't do that to me!''

"He can close you down and run you out of town—if he wants to,'' Dan Ruylander said. "Let's have a look inside.''

As they entered, Rusty and the Kid were just finishing their plaintive ballad:

"... *So he died with his six-guns ablazing,*
And only two hairs on his chest.''

Big Barnhorst sat at a bottle-littered table with a girl on his knee, and Kiowa Kempter reclined on a couch with a glass on his broad chest and his black Indian head resting on the lap of another woman. Kid Antrim and Rusty Fergus were laughing and jesting with a couple of the girls, while the rest of Imogene's staff sprawled about in a dazed stupor induced by drink, lack of sleep, and nervous exhaustion.

"You men are under arrest,'' Dan Ruylander said, thumbing the star on his vest and drawing his Colt before the Rafter celebrants could speak or move. "Come on peaceful now and damn quick. We've got orders to shoot if you don't.'' Jud Crater's gun was on them too, and the Wyoming boys stared at the badges and weapons with dull drunken amazement. Kid Antrim said: "Can't leave yet. Ain't had a go at Imogene.''

119

"I want my money first!" shouted Idaho Imogene. "Look at what they done to my place. See all that busted furniture. Look at my poor little girls. I want a thousand dollars, and that ain't half enough!"

Dan Ruylander was writing a check, after assaying the damage. "You'll take two hundred, or Sunderlee will shut you up tight."

"That's too much, Danny," protested Rusty Fergus, strapping on his gun belt. "We paid for our drinks and—our fun. Most of it anyway. The damage won't go over a hundred."

"And it was done in protecting the virtue of these fair ladies," declared Kid Antrim. "We don't really owe Madam Imogene a goddamn thing."

Imogene took ponderous backhanded swipes at the Kid and Rusty, and they ducked and dodged away laughing in delight as she railed and ranted at them. "Ain't she pretty when she's mad?" the Kid said.

"That's right, lawman, we paid our way here," Barnhorst said. "If we owe anything it's just for what's busted up. And that ain't a helluva lot more than you'd expect in a joint like this on the friging Fourth of July."

Dan crumpled up the first check, wrote another for a hundred dollars, and handed it to the hulking matron. Imogene shrieked and clawed at his face with obscene cries, but Dan warded her off and two of the girls held her in restraint. "This check probably ain't worth the goddamn paper it's wrote on!" yelled Imogene.

"Tear it up then, Idaho," drawled big Barney, grinning from his towering height. "Don't give it no chance to bounce."

"Come on, you boys. Get moving!" Jud Crater ordered, waving his pistol at them. "Outside and on your way. Straight to the jailhouse."

"We ain't broken any laws, you old buzzard," Kid Antrim said, in mock anger. "That calaboose'll never hold this crew.''

"Break out and get shot dead, if you want to,'' Jud growled. ''Get along, you drunken rabble.''

"You got no authority to call us names, old man,'' said Rusty Fergus.

"This gun's all the authority I need, sonny,'' Jud said, gesturing at Kiowa Kempter who was slowly getting untangled from his girl. ''Come on, you big half-breed. You're going too, goddamn you.''

Kempter glared savagely at him. ''You'll answer for that, you dried-up little pack-rat!'' He shouldered past Jud with a somber wink, and they all filed out, leaving Idaho Imogene raving vituperatively in the shambles of her parlor, surrounded by her weary drooping little girls.

In the street Antrim and Fergus started whooping it up with wild hilarity, until Dan Ruylander said: ''Act like you're under arrest, or Imogene's apt to put a slug in your backs.''

"Bunch of parlor-house punks,'' grumbled Jud Crater, in disgust. ''That was a pretty sight to see back there. You're a disgrace to the Rafter brand, for chrisake.''

Rusty Fergus laughed. ''That's what you get for working us on Independence Day, see? Old Abe Lincoln freed the slaves in this country.''

"Let's hit the Powder Horn,'' said Kid Antrim. ''I need a few good drinks to taper off on.''

"We're all going to taper off in the saddle, Kid,'' said Dan Ruylander. ''Plenty of work left to do back on the North Powder. We'll get something to eat and then hit the road for camp.''

The Kid and Rusty moaned in unison, but by the time they neared the jailhouse they were singing again, the blond and the redhead leaning together:

"Whoopee ti yi yo, git along little dogies,
For you know Wyoming will be your new home."

"Ain't it wonderful to be young and foolish?" sighed Jud Crater.

"You ought to know, Jud," rumbled Kiowa Kempter. "Being well along in your second childhood."

In the sheriff's office Dan and Jud returned the badges, and Sunderlee gazed at the four culprits in sour steady sorrow. "Ought to lock 'em up but I hate to clutter up the cells. Get 'em out of town and I'll forget it, Ruylander. How much you pay Imogene?"

"A hundred dollars," Dan said. "She only wanted a thousand."

"She would," Sunderlee said. "A hundred ought to cover it. That big bitch is rich enough anyway. Miss Sue Terrell was looking for you, Ruylander. Couldn't locate her brother neither. Said she was heading home to Triangle."

"Thanks, Sheriff," said Dan. "We're riding out as soon as we get some grub. I guess Garry's safe enough in Baker."

Sunderlee nodded glumly. "If Silk Coniff ain't around. You boys didn't see nothing of him, I take it? Well, I hope he's bound for Wyoming. And I can't help hoping you buckaroos will be on your way home pretty soon, too. Maybe I'm getting too old for this job."

"We'll be moving out within a week," Dan Ruylander promised, smiling. "I know how you feel, Sheriff."

"It ain't that I don't like you boys," Sunderlee said mournfully. "But I got this goddamn job and I'm a mite too old to like trouble."

122

Sixteen

Back in camp Rafter finished the branding and made a final tally of the stock, and settled down to make last careful preparations for the long trail drive east. Dan Ruylander's moment of decision was approaching, and he was far from happy about it. He hated to double-cross the Terrells, but he could not defy his own father.

Garry Terrell and his sister Sue had definitely decided to make the drive now, taking along five Triangle hands and the cook to round out the Rafter crew. Hawk Fallon was going with his four followers: Chill Cahoon, Pike Urbom, Vern Winslett, and Otis Sowerby. The cook, Smitty, wanted to get back to Wyoming and his old home on the Greybull in Big Horn Basin, once more before he died.

With the six Rafter men, the outfit would have twelve active riders to handle the herd and the remuda, while Smitty drove the chuck wagon and Sue Terrell took the wood-and-bed wagon. Each rider had a string of eight horses, including cow, rope, cut, and night ponies, especially adapted to and drilled in their particular fields of work. Garry Terrell refused to let Ruylander pay for the mounts.

"When you get home, Dan," he said, "you can buy the ones you want, and we'll dispose of the rest as we see fit."

"But I don't see why you should do that, Garry," said Dan.

"Because I want to," Terrell insisted, with quiet firmness.

The last few days were spent in further training of the

broncs, and repairing harnesses, tents, and tarpaulins. In checking equipment, shoeing horses, washing clothes, mending gear, and other more or less domestic duties. Guns had to be cleaned and oiled, along with other equipment, and the wagons had to be greased and readied for the road. Lead steers were selected and belled, and the expedition was about set to hit the trail.

Triangle retired to the home spread for last-minute preparations and farewells, with Terrell leaving replacements to help Rafter hold the cattle and the horses. On the day before departure, Dan Ruylander and old Jud Crater rode unhappily into Baker City to pull the coup they were both dreading.

"Don't see no other way out, Danny," said Crater, chewing morbidly on his tobacco. "Can't go against old Dirk's orders. It ought to work all right. You being so friendly with the Terrells, the banker ain't apt to suspect anything. He won't see Garry anyway, until they get home from Wyoming—if they ever do."

"I don't like it, Jud."

"I don't neither, Dan. Kinda taken a fancy to them Terrell kids. Can't stomach their hired hands, but Garry and Sue are real folks."

"That's the hell of it," Dan Ruylander said.

"And that gal," Crater said, spitting with the wind. "You ought to be marrying that gal, instead of stealing a goddamn herd off her. I don't know what old Dirk's thinking of, pulling a deal like this. The ones that harmed him are dead and buried, and Dirk ought to leave it lay. Kids ain't to blame for what their father and mother done."

Dan nodded miserably. "True, Jud. But I either got to cross them or Dirk—and I sure can't cross my own dad. Even if he's wrong."

"Reckon not, Dan. It's a helluva proposition any way you look at it. Maybe been better all around if Silk Coniff had got away with that money."

"Maybe so, Jud," said Dan. "It's sure a mess this way."

In town they racked their mounts in front of Kartmell's Carriage Shop, walked past the alley in which Haydock and Klugstad had died, and entered the buff brick bank shortly before closing time. Mason Werle himself came forth with a cordial greeting, inquiring as to their progress on the North Powder and asking for Sue and Garry.

"Everything's fine, Mr. Werle," said Dan Ruylander. "We're pulling out in a few days now. Garry says he can use the cash, so I want to draw the balance and close the account. Except for a hundred dollars, in case a few small checks haven't been cleared. I don't think there are any out, but there may be some little ones."

"All right, Mr. Ruylander. I'll attend to it for you myself. If that hundred isn't required, I'll mail a check to your home address. It has been a pleasure to do business with you. It's always a privilege to deal with friends of the Terrells. Yes sir, they are one of our oldest and finest families."

"You can't beat them," Dan agreed. "And I appreciate your kindness, Mr. Werle."

A few minutes later they walked out of the bank, and Dan Ruylander felt like the worst kind of thief—even though it was Rafter money in his pocket. He had turned in his check book, the draft for $45,000 already have been made out in favor of Garry Terrell. And Dan was sweating from the ordeal, his ears rimmed with fire and his cheeks flushed from shame. A rotten way to do business. When he got home, Dan was going to talk his father into paying for the herd. A profit of nearly $15,000 was enough for Rafter.

They crossed the street toward the Great Northwest House. Dan had told Jud about Garry and Sadie McLain, and he meant to find out if she was still in

Baker. Before the hotel they met Sheriff Sunderlee, and Dan inquired about the girl.

"The lady left town," Sunderlee said. "Maybe you'll see her somewhere along your way home though. And Silk Coniff too. That ain't saying they're together. Just a notion of mine, son."

They shook hands and said goodbye to the sheriff, dropped into the Powder Horn for a drink or two, bought some extra shells and whiskey for the already well-stocked wagons, and rode back toward Triangle and the North Powder River. The sun was reddening as it descended toward the Blue Mountains, and Dan thought of the western sweep of Oregon beyond that range.

"Wish we could have seen more of this country, Jud," he said. "The Columbia and The Dalles, the Willamette and the Cascades and the Pacific Coast."

"Maybe you will someday," Crater murmured. "You got a lot of time."

"Sometimes I wonder . . . ."

"If Dirk and me lived this long, you ought to be around quite a stretch yet, son. But it don't pay to think about it. A man never knows when his number's coming up."

"Just a bad feeling I've got," Dan mused. "That some of us'll never see Wyoming again."

"What the hell kinda talk is that?" snapped Jud Crater, with a disgusted splash of tobacco juice. "Get off it, kid. A man's asking for it when he starts thinking that way."

Dan Ruylander laughed softly. "I'm all right, Jud. I'm not scared, but you can't help wondering some."

"You figure Garry and Sue know about their old man and Dirk?"

"I don't think so, but I'm not sure."

"Well, we'll have trouble with Fallon and them other gunnies," Jud Crater said, with a sigh. "Have to watch 'em all the way, Danny. We stopping at Triangle?''

"No, Garry's coming up to camp tonight," Dan said. "I'll give him the check there."

"Funny they never talk much about their folks. You ever hear anything?"

"Not much, Jud," said Dan. "Once Sue mentioned that they weren't too happy, in spite of all they had here."

Crater nodded. "One way or another, kid, people generally get paid off what's coming to 'em."

In full darkness they passed the wrangler and his *caviada*, as they called the horse herd out in these parts, and then the box canyon with night-riders patrolling the mouth and the cattle lowing within the shadowy depths. The moon emerged in the east above the peaks of Idaho, and the line camp lay ahead, the cabin and corrals, the sheds and wagons and piled gear stained with firelight. This place had become homelike in the past month, and Dan was surprised to find that he vaguely regretted leaving it.

At the fireside Garry Terrell and Hawk Fallon were lounging with the stolid Indian-faced Kempter, as Dan Ruylander swung off his big gray gelding and handed the reins to Jud Crater by the corral. Terrell smiled and spoke, as Dan walked into the wavering ruddy rim of light around the campfire, and Kiowa lifted a great hand and said, "How, Chief," but Hawk Fallon neither said anything nor looked at him.

"Come in the cabin a minute, Garry," said Dan.

A lamp glowed on the rude table, and Dan got out a bottle and poured two drinks. "To our trail drive, Dan," said Terrell, raising his glass. "The old Oregon Trail in reverse." The glasses emptied, Dan Ruylander handed him the $45,000 check.

"No hurry about this, Dan," protested Garry Terrell, with some embarrassment. "Too late to bank this now. Why don't you tear it up and wait until we deliver the herd at Rafter? We're sharing the responsibility for that delivery, on our own initiative and free will. We'll accept payment when we get to Wyoming." He tried to hand his check back.

Dan waved it off. "I want you to keep it, Garry. I want to pay for something here, goddamn it! The cattle are ours now and the money is yours. Should've given it to you sooner, but it slipped my mind."

"All right, Dan." Terrell folded the check thoughtfully. "It wasn't necessary, but I'll keep it to seal the deal—if you insist?"

"I do, Garry." Ruylander was busy building a cigarette, feeling more like a criminal than he had in the bank.

"Well, I guess we're ready to roll in the morning."

"All set for the road."

Terrell grinned like a boy. "You don't know what this means to Sue and me, Dan. A trip we've planned on since we were kids. She wants to see you tonight, if you aren't too tired to come to the ranch."

Dan shook his sun-streaked sandy head. "Sorry, but I'm going to hit the blankets early." He couldn't face Sue Terrell this evening. He didn't know how he was going to face her tomorrow. And all those days and weeks, those summer months on the trail.

"Good idea for all of us, Dan," said Terrell, smiling and punching him lightly on the arm. "We'll be riding home to roll in ourselves. See you at sunup."

Hawk Fallon stood up as they came out of the log hut, his golden eyes fixed hot with hatred on Ruylander. "He's coming with us, Garry?" Fallon laughed as Terrell's dark head turned negatively. "Sometimes these Wyoming sonsabitches show some sense." He wheeled away to the horses, with Terrell at his heels, and Dan and Kempter watched the two Triangle men mount and lope away into the night.

"That Hawk's flying for a fall," Kiowa Kempter

128

said, "Spoiling for trouble. The whole goddamn drive shapes up like a civil war. Barney and Urbon always on the brink of tangling. Cahoon and Winslett eyeing Red and the Kid with itching trigger fingers. And that hog-faced Sowerby wants something from me. Ought to be a real nice ramble across the country."

"A cross we have to bear, Kiowa," said Dan Ruylander. "But it'll cut expenses some."

"They been too generous right along, Danny. It don't ring true to my Injun ears. They'll cut expenses, yeah—and maybe our throats." Kempter shrugged his massive shoulders. "If we don't beat 'em to it."

"Have to be ready for anything, Indian," said Dan. "Where are the other boys?"

"Pondosa. Barney promised to get the kids back early."

Jud Crater came bowlegged up from the corral, and the three of them sat around the fire smoking and waiting for their companions to return. Dan Ruylander was deep in thought. There was more here than met the eye. Something that didn't quite add up or make sense, on the surface of it. The Terrells might not be as innocent as they seemed. They could be playing a deeper darker game than anyone suspected.

Garry was a lot smarter or a lot dumber than he appeared, and perhaps Sue was involved in some scheme with her brother. You must expect anything from the offsprings of a man like Owen Terrell. And even if the Terrells were on the level, Hawk Fallon and the other Triangle riders were bound to stir up some sort of ruckus.

All in all, as Kiowa Kempter prophesied, it looked like a lovely trip. *On the way out we had the Silk Coniff trio to contend with,* Dan Ruylander thought. *All the way home we'll have Triangle on our necks. Not to mention storms and river crossings, heat and drought and plagues, stampedes and lags, rustlers and wolves and Indians.*

In a way though, it would be a relief if the Terrells did try to pull something dishonest and treacherous. Then Dan Ruylander could throw down on them, without any shame, compunction or remorse.

When the Rafter boys rode in they halted at the fireside, and Dan saw that they were stone sober.

"The news just came that President Garfield was shot on July second," big Barnhorst said. "Didn't kill him but they don't expect him to last long. Some crackpot named Guiteau done it."

"If Garfield dies, a gent named Arthur will be President," said Kid Antrim. "The Vice President that Foy said nobody knew."

They exchanged grave wondering glances in the fire glare, and thought of little Eddie Foy in that hotel barroom in Boise, Idaho. The three riders jogged on to the corrals, and Jud Crater spat into the glowing red embers.

"That little joker's fortune-teller sure called the turn," Jud said, wagging his lean gray head. "Now ain't that a helluva note?" He reached for the saddlebags at his side and pulled out a bottle. "It's enough to drive a man to drink."

Seventeen

In the early grayness of a July morning, Smitty set forth with his Moline chuck wagon, packed with provisions and jingling utensils, and Sue Terrell drove after him in the huge Schuttler, loaded with firewood and bedrolls, luggage and extra gear. The drive was on.

Dan Ruylander and Garry Terrell pulled out the

belled lead steers to build up their point, stringing it out with expert ease and setting the herd in motion. Jud Crater led the swing riders on the left, and Hawk Fallon directed the flankers on the right wing. Big Barnhorst and Otis Sowerby brought up the drag, and Vern Winslett was wrangling the remuda. They would shift positions and swap jobs as the drive progressed, but that was the way they started out from the North Powder, throwing the herd onto the road in a southerly course.

Astride his gray claybank at the point, Dan Ruylander found it good to be on the move at last, with the dust boiling up around the red cattle and horsemen to cloud the misty morning air. The sun cleared the mountain pinnacles of Idaho in the eastern distance, and the Blues ranged along on the western horizon. This was different from other drives Dan had participated in. These shorthorns were plump, stolid and uniformly red, in contrast to the lean fiery and vari-colored longhorns of Texas. And the crew was split down the middle into two hostile factions. Rafter against Triangle, Wyoming against Oregon. The enmity had been there since their first meeting in the Powder Horn Saloon at Baker City.

The lead steers had been chosen with care, and the stock moved along well for the first day out. The Durhams took more driving and less cutting back than Texas steers. When Dan dropped back on the flank, Rusty Fergus told him the critters needed plenty of pushing, and in the smothering dust of the drag Barney said you had to keep chousing and prodding them all the time.

Since the Fourth, Dan hadn't seen too much of Sue Terrell. He had been too busy for one thing, and a sense of guilt and shame made him avoid her as far as possible for another. And Garry hadn't mentioned Sadie McLain since that drunken night in town, although otherwise he had been as close, friendly, and considerate as ever. It was a sensitive subject, of course:

A man in love with an unworthy woman. Dan still didn't know just what to think of the Terrells. He knew that Hawk Fallon was his enemy to the death, but he wasn't sure where Garry and Sue stood in this complicated situation. With the duplicity of Owen Terrell in mind, it was natural to distrust his children, regardless of how forthright, intimate, and honest they seemed.

But Rafter was homeward bound with a herd of three thousand shorthorns and white-faces, at any rate. Starting out to follow in reverse the old Oregon Trail established by the pioneers nearly a half-century before. The Durham descendants of emigrant stock brought west in the '40s and '50s, were plodding back over the same trace their forebears had taken to reach this country.

They covered about fifteen miles per day, making their second camp on Burnt River, another Oregon tributary of the Snake. There Kiowa Kempter improvised some gunnysack nets, in which trout were caught for Smitty to cook for supper. After a beef diet the fish tasted delicious, and the big Indian and gnarled balding little Smitty came in for a good deal of half-derisive commendation and praise. But there was no mingling of the two crews, the line of demarcation clear and sharp between Rafter and Triangle, the hatred putting a cold constraint on the encampment.

Night watch on the bed grounds consisted of four reliefs of two men each, working from eight to ten, ten to twelve, midnight to two, and two to four o'clock in the morning. The nighthawks sang low mournful ballads as they slowly circled the herd: *Dan Tucker* . . . *Saddle Ole Spike* . . . *Hell Among the Yearlings* . . . *Sally Gooden* . . . *Utah Carl* . . . *Little Joe, the Wrangler* . . . *Sam Bass* . . . *The Dying Cowboy.*

When Dan Ruylander settled down in his blankets that night on Burnt River, he could hear the faint sad

lilting voices of Rusty Fergus and Kid Antrim on the
ten-to-midnight shift:

"My pard was an honest young puncher,
Upright, straightforward and square,
But he turned to a gunman and gambler,
And a woman drove him there . . . .

. . . All night long we trailed him,
Through mesquite and chaparral,
And I thought of that no-good woman,
As I saw him pitch and fall."

In the gray fog of morning, up before dawn, they
huddled around Smitty's fire to gulp hot strong
Arbuckle coffee and eat breakfast. Then they roped out
and saddled their horses, some of the broncs bucking
and pitching under the cold leather when the riders
swung aboard. Before daybreak the wagons were on the
road, and the herd was stringing out in motion,
southeast now toward the Snake River Canyon.

The sun came up, a flaming ball over the Rockies,
brightening the sky and laying elongated shadows on the
dewy earth. By midforenoon they were soaked and
sweltering in the saddle, the sun soaring and blazing
with blast-furnace heat, the dust surging up thick and
acrid from the trampling hoofs. A slow ponderous mass
churning across the scorched summer landscape, the
cattle bawling and the men yelling and cursing in that
monstrous welter. Blinded by glaring light and hailing
dirt, glued fast in the scalding wet leather, the riders
chewed tobacco to cut the dust and ease the gritty
dryness of mouth and throat. *Git along little dogies, git*
along cow critters, For you know Wyoming will be your
new home.

It took them six days to reach the ford in the Snake
River, one of the few places in which that tumultuous
stream could be crossed, at a distance of about one

hundred miles from the line camp on the North Powder. Deep in its sheer-walled canyon, racing swift and white, turbulent and treacherous in most places, the Snake looked absolutely impassable, but old Jud Crater said: "Herds have crossed here, and we can throw this one across, by Jesus."

They made the dangerous crossing somehow without loss, the men working like maniacs, wearing out one horse after another as they fought the river current and the massed beef in the raging torrent of the Snake. "Thank God that one's behind us, boys," said Jud Crater, everyone echoed those heartfelt sentiments . . . . Spent to near-exhaustion from that tremendous effort, they pushed the stock on through the wicked heat of barren lava-beds, to bivouac again at Fall Creek, a small stream that spilled over high rimrock into the deep gorge of the wide-looping Snake River. They were in Idaho now, with the whole vast mountainous breadth of the territory before them.

Restless that evening, despite his weariness, Dan Ruylander wandered away from the campfires and stood watching the slender white-spumed waterfall, glistening brilliantly in the moonbeams as it cascaded into the great canyon. The coolness of its spray felt fresh and clean on his bared head and sun-blackened face, and Dan sighed with relief and pleasure. The tension of the drive was building up daily. In a week it had become almost insupportable. The toil itself was tough and trying enough, without the added burden of Hawk Fallon's murderous hatred. Without the constant threat of death from Fallon and his associates. It was hell to conduct a trail drive, with half the men behind you looking for a chance to put a bullet into your back. That rotten crowbait sonofabitch Fallon, he thought.

Sensing, rather than hearing, someone behind him, Dan Ruylander turned and saw Sue Terrell walking toward him in the misted silvery night. Even in rough range garb she was wholly feminine, high-breasted and strong-hipped, moving with fluid grace. All Dan's hunger for her flooded back, deeper and more urgent than before.

"What's the matter, Dan?" she asked, tilting her dark head back and looking gravely up at him with quizzical blue eyes. "You've been staying away from me—ever since the Fourth."

"No, I haven't, Sue. Hasn't been time for anything but work."

"You worried about the herd?"

"Well, it's the biggest job I ever tackled."

Sue smiled with crinkling eyes. "We'll make it all right, Dan."

"Sure, we'll make it."

"But there's something wrong. Is it Fallon?"

Dan grinned bleakly. "He doesn't help matters much, Sue."

"You wish he hadn't come, don't you?" she said sharply. "You don't really want us. You wish we'd all stayed home."

"Why no, no I don't," Ruylander said. "It's not that at all, Sue. I don't know . . ."

"Oh, Dan," she murmured, her eyes shining softly, her mouth full and pleading, the flawless line of her lifted chin and throat taking his breath away. "Don't keep away from me. Don't leave me alone."

Sue swayed forward and Dan's arms went around her in honest unleashed desire. Her own arms clinging hard, she raised her ripe lips until his mouth closed down and crushed them. Dan could feel the firm fullness of her breasts, her body and thighs against him, and he wanted her more than ever. He could have her too, she was his for the taking. *And I ought to take her, like Owen took Melinda,* he thought. But he couldn't do it. Not with a girl like Sue. She was too sweet and nice, clean and decent.

Curbing and restraining his need, Dan Ruylander held her with gentle tenderness. There was nothing else then but the singing fire in their blood, the rapture of flesh and spirit, and a full-blooming wonder that filled the desert night and blurred the stars overhead.

They found a mossy bed under cedar and larch trees, and sat down shoulder to shoulder, silent and awed by this miracle that had come to them on the lofty rim of Snake River Canyon. There was no sense in denying it. They were meant for one another, blended and fitted beautifully together, and had been from the moment they met. And even before that. But a thirty-year-old feud lay between them like a double-edged blade of steel.

They were embracing in the shadows, when Hawk Fallon's voice trumpeted out from camp in brassy anger: "Ruylander! Where the hell are you, Wyoming? It's time for you to go on watch."

Dan Ruylander rose, lifting the girl alongside of him, and they walked back toward the firelit wagons and stacked equipment. "He's right, I'm due at the bed grounds," Dan said. "But I don't like his way of telling me."

"Don't have any more trouble with him, Dan," said Sue Terrell, shivering slightly at his side. "He's wicked with a gun."

"It'll come sometime, Sue," Dan said simply.

Kiowa Kempter moved forward to meet them, leading saddled night horse from the rope corral. "I'll stand your hitch, Danny," he said, bulking wide and solid against the fire glow.

"Like hell you will!" Hawk Fallon said. "Let him take his turn. He's no better than the rest of us."

Kiowa Kempter moved forward to meet them, leading a saddled night horse from the rope corral. "I'll stand

"I'll take it, Kiowa," said Dan Ruylander, reaching for the reins and glancing at Fallon. "You run your crew and let me run mine.''

Hawk Fallon laughed, with a harsh jeering note. ''Everybody works on this drive, Ruylander. Even a big augur like you. I don't like to see a trail boss tromp on his hands.''

Dan stared steadily at him. ''If you want it, Fallon, we'll have it right here. Sue, take a walk around the wagons.''

''I can't fight you on the job,'' Fallon said. ''I got my orders, and you heard 'em. Which is what makes you so brave, no doubt.''

''Then don't be making fight talk.''

''I'll talk as I damn well please, Wyoming.''

''I don't think so,'' Dan Ruylander drawled. ''You'll keep your tongue off me and my men, or you'll stand up and fight.''

Fallon's laugh was light and mocking. ''Don't be in a hurry, boy. I'm going to kill you at the end of this drive.''

''Keep your mouth shut or you won't have to wait that long,'' Dan Ruylander said mildly, and wheeled to the stark wide-eyed girl. ''Sue, you'd better get some sleep. Nothing's going to happen here. And Injun, thanks for getting me a horse.''

Dan stepped into the saddle and rode out toward the bed grounds of the drowsing herd, and Fallon gazed after him with vicious hawk eyes.

Sue Terrell disregarded Fallon to take Kempter's brawny arm, and Kiowa escorted the girl to her Sibley tent. The Indian was returning after his bedroll, when the squat Otis Sowerby came around the rear end of the Schuttler wagon and bulled into him, grinding an elbow into Kempter's belly, and snarling: ''You half-breed bastard!''

Grunting and reacting with instinctive speed, Kiowa shouldered Sowerby off and struck savagely at the ugly froglike face. Sowerby's shaggy head jerked far back under the smashing impact of the iron fist, and he went down rolling like a barrel against the wagon wheel. Pike Urbom was heaving up from his blankets, as Sowerby twisted away from the wheel and scrabbled up on stumpy legs, grabbing for his holster. Kempter's gun was half-drawn and Urbon had halted uncertainly, when the inrushing hammer of hoofs froze them motionless, a tense tableau etched in firelight and shadows.

It was Garry Terrell, coming in from his tour of duty on night patrol, and a Colt gleamed in his hand as he reined up in a sliding stop. "That's enough, boys! Let go of that gun, Otis. And you, Pike, get back into bed. You know my orders."

"He hit me," panted Otis Sowerby, thick palm smearing blood from nose and mouth across his heavy bulging jaws. "Sonofabitch slugged me."

"You started it, Otis," said Terrell. "I saw you bump into Kempter and give him the elbow. He should've hit you harder. Next time you try anything like that you're done."

Pike Urbom went back to his blankets, and Sowerby hauled out his bedding and unrolled it beside Urbon, grumbling under his breath.

"Sorry, Kiowa," said Garry Terrell, sheathing his pistol.

A rare grin creased Kempter's craggy Indian face. "I been wanting to do that for some time. Glad he gave me the chance. A pleasure to oblige a bastard like Sowerby. Any time he asks for it."

"But you'll drop it now, won't you?"

"Sure, it's dropped," Kiowa Kempter said, with gruff kindliness, "Until he comes at me again."

Eighteen

The Weiser River, swollen by mountain rains, was running high and wide when they reached it the next afternoon, a turgid yellow floodtide laced with dirty froth and streaked with driftwood. They hadn't anticipated any trouble here, but it was going to be even rougher than crossing the Snake. The time to cross was now, with the westering sun at their backs. If they waited until morning the rising sun would be in the eyes of the cattle.

"Deeper than the Snake was," Dan Ruylander said. "Have to ferry the wagons and swim the stock."

"Get the axes out," called Jud Crater, eyeing the cottonwoods along the bank. "You muscle men get your exercise right here." He selected four trees, while the strong-arm boys of both crews shed their gun belts and stripped to the waist.

Big Barnhorst and Kiowa Kempter of Rafter, and Pike Urbom and Otis Sowerby for Triangle. Swinging the axes with power and precision, making the chips fly in constant streams, they turned it into a contest as usual. Barney exulted in the flowing play of his great muscles, smiling sweatily at every stroke of the ax, but it was the blocky sober Kempter who brought his tree crashing down ahead of the others. "Injun cuttum more trees than white man ever see," Kiowa said, his broad shoulders and chest heaving and sweat-polished.

The cottonwoods felled, the branches were quickly stripped, and two trunks were lashed beneath each of the wagons. Riders swam their mounts to the opposite shore, with long ropes attached to the Moline and

Schuttler, and the vehicles were launched and rafted over on log floats in a slow wallowing arc, the current carrying them downstream and across with the aid of horse-drawn lines. The wagons and the cavvy safely across, all hands shucked off guns and superfluous clothing and saddle gear, in preparation for the major task.

Dan Ruylander and Garry Terrell pulled out the lead steers and put them into the water, and the herd poured after them with Jud Crater and Hawk Fallon and their swing riders pushing hard on the flanks. The lead animals plunged out after the point men, until they were beyond their depth and swimming in the strong current. Swing and drag riders combined to keep the beef streaming over the bank into the water.

Swimming their horses on the downstream side, Dan and Garry kept the leaders going, lashing out with wet ropes at the short-horned heads and brute faces. Until the point was wading once more, climbing out of the far shallows onto dry ground, prodded on by Dan and Garry to make room for the followers. Sue Terrell and Smitty had mounted ponies to hold the stock there, while Dan and Garry splashed back into the river to keep the herd moving.

The swimming cattle, current-dragged into an ever deepening loop downstream, were held in a ragged floundering arc by cowboys with slashing quirts and rope ends. It was a ceaseless and savage struggle between mounted men and beasts. Occasionally the line was broken by rampaging driftwood, uprooted from the banks upriver, and the cows would have yielded to panic and the current at such times, if it hadn't been for the swimming horses and shouting flailing men. It was a fight all the way to keep the critters moving. It went on and on in a churning watery chaos, as the sun lowered redly in the west and light dimmed upon the land and the embattled Weiser.

At last the drag was entering the river, choused and driven by Kiowa Kempter and two Triangle men, Otis Sowerby and Pike Urbom. On the far eastern shoreline, Dan Ruylander and Barnhorst had switched wet saddles onto fresh broncs. Glancing across to check on the drag, Dan was suddenly impelled to throw his new mount back into the stream, and big Barney was close behind him. Surging and splashing they swam their horses out to meet the tail-end of the herd, whipping at red and white cow faces as they went to maintain that unbroken loop of beef.

It happened in midstream, while Dan and Barney were still some distance away, and details were lost in the brawling confusion and dusky light. A large timber came rocketing down on the boiling muddy tide, and Dan and Barney yelled until their throats split: "Look out above! Break the line and let it through! Break 'em up, Injun!"

Kiowa Kempter fought furiously to breach the wall of swimming stock, but it refused to give. Already the snag-roots of the tree were clawing the cattle into crazed panicky terror. Then a bawling steer's back broke beneath the smash of that huge trunk, and its neighboring creatures milled and thrashed about in utter foaming confusion and fear.

"Pull out, Injun!" screamed Dan Ruylander, his cry shredded and lost in the bellow of animals and the endless roar of the river. *Too late,* Dan thought, in horror and despair. *Kiowa'll never get out.*

But Kempter was swinging his big roan around, and breaking his way clear of that whirling maelstrom, when he collided with another horse and rider—Otis Sowerby. Drifting entangled in showers of spray, there was a vicious blurred motion on Sowerby's part, and Kiowa rocked in his saddle. Dan couldn't be certain, but it looked as if Sowerby had quirted the Indian across the face. Steers were drifting downstream now, drowned or drowning, and Dan's view of the scene was obscured except for brief glimpses.

It seemed that Pike Urbom drove his mount toward the other pair, and they merged momentarily in a spray-screened welter. A quirt and an arm rose high and flashed downward, and it looked like Urbom striking at Kempter with the loaded butt of his whip. But again Dan was not sure. A turmoil of interlocked cows floating downcurrent blocked Dan's vision entirely then, and when the way cleared again Kiowa Kempter was gone, his riderless roan plunging down the river with a small batch of injured, frenzied and drowning cattle.

There was no time, no chance whatever to save the big Indian. Nothing to do but try to hold the rest of the drag, and push the short-horns on across the torrential Weiser. Fighting like madmen, Ruylander and Barnhorst with Urbom and Sowerby, managed to do this and complete the crossing. But a man and a horse and a dozen or so cows had gone down the river, and Kiowa Kempter must be dead for he couldn't swim a single stroke. The big Injun was gone.

They searched the stream and both shorelines until darkness closed in, but found no trace of Kempter. "He's in the Snake by now," Barnhorst said, with soft bitterness. "That goddamn river got the Injun after all."

"Did you see it the way I did, Barney?" asked Dan Ruylander.

"I reckon so, Dan," said Barnhorst. "They put the Injun under. And I'm going to kill them. Every last frigging bastard!"

"Not yet, Barney. We need them to finish the drive. We'll have to wait."

"Wait?" Barnhorst said, through gritted teeth. "Wait for the sonsabitches to kill us all off, one by one?"

"We'll take them—when the times comes, Barney," said Dan. "But not now—not tonight."

"I don't know, Dan, if I can hold myself back."

Drenched, shivering and sick, they reached the east bank where camp was being set up. Sowerby and Urbom were drying themselves by the fire, and Smitty was working at the hinged tailgate of his chuck wagon. The others were still hunting for Kempter, or out with the herd and the remuda.

Slipping from waterlogged saddles, Ruylander and Barnhorst walked toward the fire. They were still unarmed, but the Triangle men hadn't donned their guns either. Urbom and Sowerby got up warily at their approach.

"What happened out there?" Dan Ruylander demanded.

"Kempter went under," Sowerby muttered sullenly. "We tried to save him, but—"

"You quirted him, you lying sonofabitch!" Dan said.

"He was trying to drag me down with him. I had to do something."

Dan whirled on the tall Urbom. "And you finished him, you bastard!"

Pike Urbom shrugged his high shoulders. "It was him or Otis. The Injun was crazy scared, out of his head. He might've got us all killed there."

"That's a goddamn lie!" Dan Ruylander said, with quiet deadliness. "You're liars and murderers, and you're going to answer for it."

"They're going to die for it, Danny," said Barnhorst, his face and eyes terrible in the firelight. Striding to a horse tethered nearby, a dry horse with dry gear, Barney ripped the carbine out of its scabbard. Wheeling back and jacking a shell into the chamber, he held the carbine on the Triangle pair. "Right here and now."

"We ain't got guns," Sowerby protested, spreading his palms.

"Go get some then," Barnhorst said, motioning with the barrel.

"No, Barney," said Dan Ruylander. "It'll have to wait. We're shorthanded enough as it is. And here comes the rest of 'em. We can't start a war here, Barney."

Hoofs clopped in the outer darkness, and horsemen straggled wearily in toward the campfire. Garry Terrell and Hawk Fallon, Jud Crater and Kid Antrim and others.

"Hold this, Dan." Barnhorst thrust the carbine at him. 'I got to do something or bust wide open!" An easy towering figure, he moved toward the Triangle men with grim purpose.

Barney's left fist lashed into Sowerby's frog-face, driving the stocky man back and down against the bole of a cottonwood. Pivoting smoothly Barnhorst caught the ducking Urbom with a ripping right hand, that dropped Pike across a windfall at the edge of the clearing.

"Get up!" Barney said, waiting with great hands clenched and ready.

Otis Sowerby shook his shag-head against the tree trunk, and Pike Urbom sat up groggily on the log, spitting blood and snarling: "We can't fight you with that carbine on us, for chrisake!"

"That's enough, Barney," said Dan. "We'll settle with them later."

"What's wrong here, Dan?" asked Garry Terrell, from his saddle, glancing from the carbine to the bleeding faces of Urbom and Sowerby, and then at Barnhorst who was rubbing his raw knuckles.

"Your boys could've saved Kiowa," said Dan Ruylander. "They didn't, Garry. In fact, they helped put him under."

"Tell it straight, Dan," grated Barnhorst. "They killed him!"

Shock showed on Terrell's handsome features, and the other wet-shining bristled faces on either side of him. "I can't believe that," Terrell said, moving his crisp dark head from side to side.

"I'm afraid it's the truth, Garry," said Dan Ruylander gently.

"Let me talk to Pike and Otis," said Terrell, dull and toneless.

"You can talk to them," Barnhorst said, with icy restraint. "We'll take care of 'em—when the time is right."

It was a long time before Dan Ruylander could sleep that night, and there were other wakeful men in the camp including big Barney. They had broken out some whiskey, but that didn't help much either.

Kiowa Kempter was gone, dead because old Dirk Ruylander insisted on trying to collect an ancient debt from enemies already in their graves. The solid, steady, rocklike Injun, somber-faced and great-hearted, the first but not the last to die on this drive. Dan's dark premonitions were beginning to come true, and he wondered who would be the next to go.

Garry and Sue Terrell were deeply sympathetic and sorrowful, but either unable or unwilling to believe that Otis Sowerby and Pike Urbom had deliberately killed Kempter. Those two now denied the earlier admission of partial guilt, that Dan had startled out of them by pretending to have witnessed clearly the entire incident. So there'd be no censure or punishment for Urbom or Sowerby, until Rafter got around to administer it.

Dan had asked Barnhorst and the rest to hold their hands until they reached the Sweetwater, but no one believed the issue would wait that long.

Nineteen

The drive rolled on in a southeasterly direction, across the sagebrush desert of a broad tableland with mountains massed against the eastern skyline. The seared plateau was marked by cruel malpais and broken with weird volcanic outcroppings, studded with lava dykes and gashed by jagged dry gulches threading toward the canyon of the Snake in the west. This country corroded flesh and ate at a man's sanity.

Relations were more strained and precarious than ever. The veiled enmity between Rafter and Triangle was out in the open now, and naked hatred and tension rode always with them. Kempter's roan returned to the remuda, but Kiowa was gone forever and his loss left a gaping hole in the Wyoming ranks. They all missed the big Injun, and Dan Ruylander couldn't help blaming his father for Kiowa's death. Barnhorst had to exercise immense restraint whenever he encountered Pike Urbom and Otis Sowerby, and Kid Antrim and Rusty Fergus were nagged and fretted by their lust to cut down the Oregon hands.

Ruylander and Jud Crater tried to keep Rafter in line, while Garry Terrell and even Hawk Fallon endeavored to curb and control the Triangle riders. But nerves and tempers hung on a hair-triggered edge, and the incessant pressure wore on everyone. One careless word or false move would surely set off a fatal explosion.

After making a dry camp on the arid tabletop, they pressed on the following day to the Payette River, too late and dark for the fording. In the town of Emmett, Dan hired a half-breed horse wrangler to take charge of the cavvy for the rest of the trip. The barking of settlement dogs kept the herd awake and restless all night, and watches had to be doubled to prevent stampeding. They made a morning crossing of the Payette before sunrise, with everybody soaking wet and snarling curses in the chill gray-fogged dimness.

In the raw chopped-up hill country between the Payette and Boise, August arrived with days that were glaring bright and blazing hot. Terrific electrical storms broke at night, with thunder booming, lightning flaring, rain turning to hail, and the cattle always on the verge of a stampede.

Outside of Boise they bedded down the herd, bathed in the river, and visited the town in relays to replenish supplies, look for mail, and get a taste of civilization once more. Dan Ruylander and Barnhorst rode in with Sue and Garry Terrell, and big Barney chanted softly:

> "We all hit town, and we hit her
>   On the fly—
> We bedded down the cattle on
>   A hill nearby . . ."

Sue Terrell went to the hotel to enjoy the luxury of a bath and a bedroom, and Garry disappeared on some quest of his own, which led Dan to wonder if Sadie McLain could be in Boise. There was some mail for Rafter, and Dan and Barney settled down in a saloon to drink beer and read their letters. There was one envelope addressed to Kempter, and Barney said with a sad smile. "That little part-Injun gal who lives with Cattle Kate, Danny. For a rough homely tongue-tied buck, old Kiowa did all right with the women."

Dan Ruylander found an encouraging paragraph in his father's letter. Old Dirk had written:

> "I've been worrying some, son. Maybe I was wrong about this whole business. Owen and Melinda are dead, and their kids may be as good and decent as my own. I hope it don't come to any shooting war

147

out there, Danny. I don't want you or any of the
boys hurt. If the Terrells are as good as you say,
maybe we ought to pay them for the herd after all."

Ruylander and Barnhorst went to a barbershop for
haircuts. Out of the chair first, Dan said he'd wait
outside. He was lounging against an awning upright and
smoking a cigar, when he saw Garry Terrell turn into an
alley across the street beside a place called the King
High. The kind of spot that Sadie McLain might be
employed in.

Sensing some menace in the night, Dan started across
the street and glimpsed another man ducking into that
alleyway after Garry. A sleek groomed figure in well-cut
town clothing, it looked like Silk Coniff. Silk wouldn't
forget that slug Garry had put into him in Baker City,
thought Dan, increasing his long-legged strides and
loosening the Colt in its leather.

The passage was empty when Dan reached the mouth,
the backyard beyond it spattered faintly with lamplight.
As Dan cleared the rear corner, the man was about to
open a back door to the King High, from which music
and laughter issued. It was unmistakably Silk Coniff,
bent on evening the score with Garry Terrell.

"Looking for somebody, Silk?" called Dan
Ruylander, poised for the draw.

Coniff spun and drew lightning-fast, the flame
spearing out with a roar, and the bullet snatched hotly
at the sleeve of Dan's jacket as his own .44 blasted
bright and loud, springing hard against his palm. The
shot spouted splinters into Silk Coniff's face, and he
lunged in through the doorway before Dan could fire
again, the door slamming shut behind him. Dan
Ruylander followed on the run, leaping onto the
platform and gripping the knob in his left hand. But the
door would not budge. Dan stepped aside and waited in
the shadows, the gun ready in his hand.

The door opened narrowly and Garry Terrell peered

148

out over a gun barrel, lowering the weapon as he recognized Ruylander. "What the hell was that, Dan?"

"Silk Coniff followed you in there, Garry."

Terrell glanced back at the interior. "He must have gone right through to the front."

"Sadie inside?"

Terrell nodded with abrupt coolness. "Correct. But you can't blame her."

"Maybe not," Dan said. "But this isn't a very safe place for you."

"I can take care of myself, Dan," said Terrell stiffly. "Thanks for the warning, but I'll handle Coniff if he tries anything more."

"All right, Garry, but don't underestimate him. Silk's good."

Garry Terrell smiled. "I'm supposed to be pretty good myself, Dan. See you back at camp."

"Sure." Dan Ruylander holstered his Colt and dropped from the platform, as Terrell closed the door in back of him. He's touchy about that girl, Dan reflected. But I guess it's only natural for a man mixed up with that kind of a woman. Sadie's probably going to follow us all the way to Wyoming. She and Silk Coniff both. Perhaps they're not traveling together, but they never seem to be very far apart.

Dan met Barnhorst in front of the barbershop and told him what had occurred, and Barney was all for hunting Silk Coniff down at once.

"To hell with it, Barney," said Dan Ruylander, after some consideration. "Let's get a drink instead. We've got enough trouble in our own camp. And Silk will give us another crack at him, sooner or later."

They forded the Boise River on sandbars, where prospectors were washing and panning for gold, and drifted the herd southeast in the glaring heat of August.

Driving on in billowing dust banners over a wild broken terrain, the riders sweat-plastered in scorching saddles, the stock inclined to wilt and lag under the merciless molten blue sky. Two days to the headwaters of Canyon Creek, and two more to the Camas. Moving almost due east now, with the Sawtooth spires ranging the northern horizon.

Garry Terrell was aloof and remote since that night in Boise, avoiding Dan Ruylander and Rafter, spending more time with Hawk Fallon and the other Oregon men. Again Dan wondered if Terrell was his friend or his enemy. Only time and the ultimate showdown would tell for certain, it seemed.

Camas Prairie, a great sea of rich gold-green grass with heavy-boughed trees shading the creek and the Smoky Mountains standing guard at the north, was a welcome respite from the intense heat and choking lava dust of the volcanic wastelands behind them. White-faced Herefords grazed here, tended by Indians of the Lemhi tribe. Fish were plentiful in Camas Creek, and they scooped them out in the bransack nets rigged earlier by Kiowa Kempter, and Smitty baked the trout in his Dutch oven to vary their diet. Garry Terrell went hunting in the Smokies and brought back a deer to supplement the beef supply with venison. The Camas, which had delighted thousands of pioneers on the Oregon Trail, was still a grand and beautiful valley, lush green and golden in the August sunshine.

But Otis Sowerby didn't like the Indians, and Terrell and Fallon had to forcibly restrain him from throwing a gun on one of them.

"For chrisake, Otis, lay off the Injuns," said Fallon.

At Jud Crater's suggestion, they slowed the pace on Camas Meadows, to let the cattle fill up well on grass and water and to give both men and animals a much-needed rest. But it all came to naught. They were at supper when a wild band of Lemhi bucks, drunk on mescal, stampeded their Herefords through the bed grounds of the trail herd, scattering short-horns far and wide all over the plain.

The next day was spent in gathering, cutting out and trimming the mixed herds, the Oregon and Wyoming riders swearing steadily at the crazy Injuns, as they wore out one bronc after another in the shimmering mid-summer heat.

Otis Sowerby, squat and ugly in the saddle, spotted a pair of young Lemhis in the brush, laughing in gleeful mockery as they watched the cowboys slave and sweat to untangle and separate the cattle. Cursing in vicious fury, Sowerby yanked out his handgun and spurred his mount straight at the thicket in which the young braves were lurking. "I'll have your red asses, by gawd!" snarled Sowerby.

Cutting out stock nearby, Kid Antrim observed this and whirled his bay gelding off in pursuit of Sowerby, yelling: "No, Otis! No, you goddamn fool, *no!*" The Kid knew what it would mean if Sowerby killed an Indian or two here. They'd have the whole tribe on top of them, and no doubt lose the trail herd and quite possibly their lives. "Sowerby! Leave them Injuns alone, man! Jesus H. Christ!"

Sowerby reined up and brought his sorrel rearing and snorting around, fire lancing back as Otis lined a shot at Antrim. The slug whipped off the Kid's hat and left it hanging by the lanyard behind his blond head. Drawing and leveling off his .44 Colt, with the bay at a full gallop Kid Antrim thought of the dead Kempter as he thumbed the hammer. Flame spurted pale in the sunlight, and the wind-flattened blast was like an echo of Sowerby's gunshot.

The bullet lifted Sowerby from the stirrups and drove him back over the cantle. He bounced from that sorrel rump in spread-eagled flight, as the horse bolted from under him, and thumped rolling to earth in a storm of

151

dust. Hard hit but still snarling and fighting, Otis Sowerby thrashed about in the trampled grass and fired at the oncoming rider. He kept firing until Kid Antrim threw down and hammered four swift shots into him, the muzzle flashes continuous and the reports blending into sustained thunder, as Sowerby's broken bulk jerked and twitched on the smoking green floor of the prairie.

Slim and whiplike in the leather, Kid Antrim pulled on his hat and began reloading his Colt, while horsemen from both crews raced toward the scene with guns in hand. Dan Ruylander was afraid the wholesale slaughter had started and nothing could stop it, but Garry Terrell reached the spot first and took a stand beside the Kid.

"It was self-defense, boys," Terrell told his men, as they pulled up around him. "Sowerby fired the first shot. I saw it and some of you saw it. Holster those guns now."

"What the hell was Antrim after Otis for?" demanded Hawk Fallon, yellowish eyes hungry on the Kid's thin face.

Garry Terrell pointed into the brush, where two young Lemhis were fleeing panic-stricken. "See those Indians? Otis was going after them with a gun, and the Kid tried to stop him. If Otis had shot those young bucks, there would have been a massacre on the Camas—with us the victims. I guess you realize that as well as I do."

"All right, Garry," said Hawk Fallon. "The Kid's clear—this time." He turned to Urbom. "Get the tools, Pike, and we'll put Otis under."

So they buried Otis Sowerby on Camas Prairie, which was more than they'd been able to do for Kiowa Kempter, and they went on cutting out, trimming and tallying the road herd. Engaging a young homesteader kid named Halley as a replacement, they drove on through foothills rich with foliage and abounding in game to Little Camas Meadows.

But the feuding and killing wouldn't stop here, Dan Ruylander knew, any more than it had with the death of Kempter. The Triangle men, Pike Urbom and Hawk Fallon in particular, would be watching and waiting for an opportunity to strike back at Rafter. Thus far the score was even, one dead on each side. Dan wondered if any of them would live to cross the Divide and reach the Sweetwater River in Wyoming.

Twenty

Beyond Big Wood River they struck lava rock country once more, charred black, sooty and evil-smelling, the giant lava beds and truncated cones of long-dead volcanos that were known as Craters of the Moon. A fantastic tortured area where no plant or animal life could exist, and the crusted hollow earth rumbled and roared under the hoofs of the cattle. Steaming hot water spouted from holes in the surface here, and ice-cold water jetted up there. The whole broken mass, honeycombed underneath and spiked with shattered peaks above, was hideous and grotesque and utterly desolate. A nightmare landscape that laid an eerie spell on man and animal alike.

Cattle strayed in this jigsaw terrain, disappearing as soon as they broke away from the herd, and sweating swearing riders, blackened and coughing from the lava dust, pursued them over jagged malpais, among huge angular dykes, and into the deep potholes. "This," said old Jud Crater, "is the country God forgot and hell wouldn't have."

"Yeah," said Barney. "It looks like hell burnt out and warmed over."

It was like another world all right, thought big Barnhorst as he spurred his soot-streaked dun after some elusive strays. A dead planet, ravaged and ruined beyond belief. It must have been really hell on earth when these ancient volcanos were erupting, blowing off their peaks in vast fiery explosions, filling the air with flame and ashes, flooding the ground with hot lava. The Injun liked to see things like this. Kiowa would have enjoyed this crazy country.

Barney was lonesome and lost without the big Indian. Nothing seemed the same with Kiowa Kempter gone, and nobody could ever take his place. Barney liked Dan and old Jud and the two kids, but they weren't as close to him as the Injun had been. The times we had together, that Injun and me, Barnhorst mused, in wistful melancholy. The fights and drunks and frolics. Never was a man like Kiowa in a roughhouse brawl. How the Injun could belt them and break them down and fling them hell-west-and-crooked all over the place. Many a saloon we cleaned out in our time. Now Kiowa was dead, rotting somewhere along the banks of the Weiser or the Snake. And Kid Antrim had settled with Sowerby, but Pike Urbom was still alive and unhurt, as cocky and strutting as ever.

The trace that Barnhorst was on led down a natural ramp of dirt-and-ash-covered stone into a dim weird maze of subterranean corridors and caverns. Barney's spine crawled cold and his neck-hairs bristled as he followed the tracks underground, wondering if three head were worth it when a man and horse might drop out of sight into bottomless holes at any minute.

A short passage opened into a great chamber beneath the surface, and Barnhorst urged his nervous mount onward with reluctance. Three red steers were drinking from a spring at the left, and over on the right was a

154

gaping black fissure from which vile steamy vapors rose and swirled. Apparently the scent of fresh cold water, penetrating even the foul mineral odors, had lured the Durhams into this unlikely place. The cavern was high and spacious. Stalactites, hanging like great ebony icicles from the lofty ceiling, reached to within ten feet of the head of a tall mounted man like Barney. Stalagmites were built up from the floor into ragged pillars, almost merging with the stalactites here and there.

Fascinated by that steaming chasm to the right, Barnhorst booted the skittish dun in that direction for a closer look. There was a hollow boiling sound from below, as if some horrible eruption might be imminent, and Barney felt a chill prickle run up his spine and tighten his scalp. The chamber stank of corruption and decay, and he wondered why the hell he didn't turn back and pick up those three critters and fan out of here fast. But something drew him toward the edge of that foggy rift in the lava.

The sudden and unreal appearance of Pike Urbom from behind a craggy aborted column, towering in the saddle with pistol in hand, froze Barnhorst's blood and backbone and raised the short hairs on the back of his neck. An awful place to die, he thought irrationally.

"So it worked," Pike Urbom said, a buck-toothed sneer twisting his vicious black-smeared face. "I hazed them steers down here, hoping one of you bastards would follow 'em. And I'm glad it was you, sucker!"

"How about an even break, Pike?" said Barnhorst. "You're supposed to be slick with a gun."

"I could take you that way too, but I ain't foolish. Why run a risk when I've got the drop? You're a dead man, Barney, and they'll never find you." Urbom motioned with his gunhand at the vapor-clouded cleft in the floor, too busy gloating to notice that Barney's dun was edging nearer to his black mount.

"Where's your guts, Pike?" taunted Barnhorst.

"That's where you're getting it, right in the guts," Pike Urbom said, deliberately bringing his gun to bear.

With a cruel rake of the spurs, Barnhorst put his rangy dun straight and hard into the black, drawing his Colt as they crashed together. The jarring collision rocked Urbon backward and jerked his gunhand high, so that his shot richocheted, screeching off the cavern roof and loosed a shower of rock fragments.

As the horses reared and circled on the impact, Barney leaned out and chopped his steel barrel across Urbom's oversized head. Bent low under the crushing blow, Pike pitched from the leather into a face-down sprawl on the stone floor, the gun flying from his grasp. Kicking out of the stirrups, Barnhorst jumped down and slapped the dun's flank to chase it along after the snorting black and out of the way. "Now you ugly sonofabitch," Barney said, turning to his adversary.

Pike Urbom was clambering slowly upright, swaying and shaking his head and groping blindly for his left-hand gun. Using his barrel like a terrible hammer again, Barney beat the man down onto all fours. Urbom should have been out but his skull must have been like iron, for he was still conscious and struggling upward. Sheathing his Colt, wanting to feel that hated flesh under his bare hands, Barnhorst strode in and smashed away left and right at the dazed evil countenance. Urbom groaned and fell backward, rolling in the sooty ashes, blood pouring from his gashed scalp and broken face.

"That's for the Injun," panted Barney. "How you like it, Pike?"

"That's enough," moaned Urbon. "Don't hit—me—again."

Once more Urbom scrambled weakly to his knees, then his feet, gasping, sobbing and pleading for mercy now. But when Barney stepped back a pace, Pike clawed left-handed for his other gun. Lunging in with renewed fury, Barnhorst lashed and hooked savagely at that crimsoned black face, feeling the buck teeth splinter and give under his knuckles as he flogged Urbom's large head from one side to the other.

Scarlet spattered Barney's forearms and Pike Urbom lurched backward, floundering and threshing on the very brink of that steam-shrouded dark crevice. Stunned and beaten as he was, Urbom saw his danger and uttered a strangled scream as he reared upright in frantic desperation and terror. Barnhorst stepped in and swung with all the power in his big rangy frame, landing left and right and feeling the shocks ripple way to his shoulders.

Beaten back off his feet, Pike Urbom toppled heavily and rolled over the rim into those odorous mists, dropping instantly from sight into the depths of the earth. One retching scream floated up through the vapor, and then there was stillness. Barney listened for some time, but never heard the body strike. That chasm must extend halfway to China, he thought. Pike Urbom was gone, as if he never had existed, and Kiowa Kempter was fully avenged now. It didn't bring the Injun back, but it was the best Barney could do for him.

Catching and mounting his dun and taking the reins of the black, Barnhorst choused the three strays out into the open and up the rocky incline. The blue sky never looked any better, and fresh air never smelled and tasted so good to Barney. He couldn't inhale enough of it.

When Barnhorst returned to the main column and reported finding Urbom's horse beside a deep hole in the lava, Hawk Fallon and the other Triangle cowboys were scornfully incredulous and raging for revenge.

"Sure, he fell into a hole—with your bullet in his back!" the Hawk jeered. "Don't give us that bullshit about finding Pike's hoss."

"Check my guns if you want to," Barney invited

calmly. "Neither the saddle gun nor the Colt has been fired. And I don't shoot in the back, Fallon."

"You killed Urbom," insisted Fallon. "I don't know or give a goddamn *how,* but you killed him. Just as sure as Antrim shot Sowerby."

"You're calling me a liar, Hawk?" inquired Barnhorst.

Hawk Fallon laughed. "You don't like it, big boy? Fill your hand then!" He threw his bronc toward Barney's dun, hand clawed by his gun butt, but Garry Terrell rode in between them with upraised palm.

"Hold on, Hawk, and back off," he commanded. "We've got to take Barney's word for this, just as we took the word of Pike and Otis that they were innocent of Kempter's death. Break it up now, boys, and get on with the drive."

"What the hell we going to do, Garry?" demanded Fallon, pulling his mount back angrily. "Hold still while they rub us out one after another, for chrisake?"

"Accidents happen on every trail drive, Hawk."

"Sure," Fallon said. "And maybe the next one'll happen to Rafter instead of Triangle. Maybe them bastards'll start dropping outa sight."

They plodded on through that bleak tormented wilderness of blasted volcanic peaks and lava rock, to cross the Big Lost River near Arco, an old stage depot and ranch. To the north the Idaho ranges—Lost River, Lemhi and Beaverhead—were ranked in pleated and serrated grandeur. The southern sky was dominated by the ruined bulk of Big Butte, at this point. Scouring black ashes were a constant torture, and nostrils and throats ached with a tight hot dryness.

"This here Lost River really gets lost," Jud Crater declared, as they splashed across it. "Keeps disappearing underground, coming out again, and finally vanishes altogether under the surface. To come out once more in a faraway canyon of the Snake as the

Thousand Springs, cold water jets spouting from a lava palisade above the river.''

"Thank you, Professor," laughed Kid Antrim. "I was beginning to think you'd lost your tongue—or maybe your mind."

Crater grunted. "This trip and the company on it would make any man lose his mind. Something you and the Redhead don't have to worry about, being without brains to begin with."

Dan Ruylander had lost track of time and distance, everything but the grinding labor of the drive and the deadly menace of the feud with Triangle. The Oregon men had to be watched with unceasing vigilance. If they didn't go for Dan, they'd try to get Kid Antrim and Barnhorst for sure. Vaguely Dan realized that August was burning away, and they were more than halfway across Idaho Territory.

They pushed on through a sunstruck wasteland of lava rock and cinder cones and filthy black dust, and Dan felt coated and corroded, inside as well as out, with gritty powdered lava. In the blistering heat every rider suffered the central split in dry chapped lower lips. A painful gash that would not heal, and was eased only by applying wet leaves of chewing tobacco. Even Sue Terrell submitted to this treatment, as a last resort to gain relief.

Sue and Smitty rode the wagons, and the Sioux breed wrangled the horse herd, while young Halley helped work the cattle. Those four were neutral, as far as Dan could tell, but he still didn't know exactly where Garry Terrell was standing. Garry had been cool and distant ever since Boise, although he did his best to maintain peace in camp. Dan thought perhaps Sadie McLain had contrived somehow to turn Terrell against him. Dan Ruylander wasn't seeing much of Sue these days and nights. Garry Terrell or Hawk Fallon always seemed to be in the way, occupying the girl's free time and shutting

Dan out.

They were approaching another ford in a deep rocky defile of the Snake River, and above this crossing was the town of Blackfoot, near Fort Hall. Dan wondered if Sadie McLain and Silk Coniff would be waiting for them in that settlement. It was more than likely.

Twenty-One

Their second crossing of the Snake, a bad one in the swift white waters of a rock-walled gorge, was made without mishap, and they bedded the herd outside of Blackfoot on a high plain east of the river canyon. In town they laid over to rest and relax and celebrate a little; to buy provisions, pick up mail, and shrink the wagon tires against expansion from desert sun and heat. Here they learned that President Garfield was still alive, but expected to die at almost any moment.

Garry Terrell disappeared for a time, and Dan Ruylander figured he was somewhere with Sadie McLain, but he did not see anything of Silk Coniff. They worked in shifts to guard the stock, releasing the off-duty members of the crew to visit the barrooms of Blackfoot or historic old Fort Hall. The men indulged in barbershop baths, shaves, and haircuts, while Sue Terrell luxuriated in the comfort and privacy of the best hotel room in town.

Sue and Dan rode out to the fort one day with Jud Crater and Kid Antrim, and old Jud told them something about the outpost: "Man named Nat Wyeth from Boston built it in 1834 to trade for furs, and across the territory Fort Boise was put up the same year. Both later was stopping places on the Oregon Trail. Your folks camped out here on their way west, Sue."

"Suppose I'll ever get to be as smart as you are, Jud?" asked Antrim, with affected wistfulness.

"It ain't likely, Kid. Unless you live to be a coupla hundred."

Kid Antrim laughed merrily, tilting his golden head. "I don't want to live to be as old as you, Jud."

"You ain't apt to neither, Kid," said Jud Crater, with a wry grin.

Dan and Sue wandered away from the others, out around the ancient bleached stockade, and the girl was silent and thoughtful.

"Thinking of your folks, Sue?" inquired Dan gently. She nodded her dark head, and he went on: "Tell me about them. What were they like?"

"They were fine, Dan. Really wonderful to Garry and me. But they—they weren't altogether happy, I guess."

"Your father died very soon after your mother, Sue?"

She bowed. "He didn't want to live—after Mother went."

Sue obviously didn't want to discuss it, and Dan switched the subject: "When we started out you said I was avoiding you. Lately you've been dodging me, it seems. Why, Sue?"

"No real reason, Dan. There's just no time or place on the trail."

"Maybe you heard something about me—in Boise?"

She smiled dimly. "Well, Dan, I know you were with Sadie McLain in Baker City, if that's what you mean."

"That was before I met you."

"You didn't have to lie about it."

"I'm sorry, Sue," said Dan Ruylander.

Sue gestured indifferently. "It doesn't matter anyway."

Anger stirred in Dan. "Your brother's probably with her right now."

"I don't doubt it, Dan," said Sue Terrell coolly. "But I can't do much about that—either. Perhaps it's all right—meant to be. If it makes Garry happy—and she doesn't hurt him too much."

"Sue," said Dan, his throat aching-full as he reached for her, but the girl drew away from him and Dan let his hands drop emptily. "Okay, Sue. We'll play it any way you want it. Let's go back and find Jud and the Kid."

The night before they were to put the herd on the road again, Garry Terrell was back and all hands were in camp. Dan Ruylander and Kid Antrim were standing the ten-to-midnight watch, slowly circling the bed grounds in opposite directions. There was a heavy ominous hush in the air, as if a storm were gathering in the night. Once when Dan met the Kid, he was singing:

> *"Finished the drive and drawn my money,*
> *Going into town to see my honey."*

The next time around, the Kid was on a more mournful strain:

> *"In a narrow grave just six by three,*
> *They laid him there on the lone prairie."*

"Storm coming, Kid," said Dan Ruylander, as they halted their horses. Thunder was muttering around distant peaks now, with vivid flashes illuminating the far horizons.

"A big one, I reckon," Antrim agreed. "And that goddamn canyon is too close and deep for comfort, Danny."

Dan nodded gravely and they went on their separate ways about the perimeter. If the cattle broke westward, they might lose the whole herd in the sunken cliff-sided gorge of the Snake River. His mount was nervous and bristling under the impending storm, and the hair of the Durhams and Herefords stood out brushlike as they stomped and shifted uneasily, aware of the coming violence. A sulphurous smell tinged the air. When the riders met again, Dan said:

"Kid, you better go in and roust out some of the boys. It's coming pretty soon and it's going to be a bad one."

"Sure, Dan. Let the lazy bastards get off their dead asses and earn their wages." Kid Antrim laughed and wheeled his night horse, kicking it into a dead run for the slumbering camp.

Dan dismounted to put on his slicker, as the thunder rolled closer and atmospheric pressure increased. Reinforcements were riding out from camp, when the storm broke suddenly and with earth-shaking fury. Lightning split the heavens in long forked flares, and thunder rumbled and crashed with the awesome sound of rock mountains disintegrating and tumbling into shattered chaos. Lurid balls of green and blue fire danced on the horned heads of the stock, until the animals bleated and surged about in terror. Rain slashed down in blinding sheets, and with it came hailstones like steel pellets, stinging and flaying bare skin and hides, hurting even through layers of drenched clothing.

"If they run, let 'em run east," Dan Ruylander said through his tight teeth. "Please God head 'em east, if they've got to break."

Dan was galloping toward the western perimeter and the Snake River, with the whole crew aroused and mounted and fanning out behind him. But the stampede started before they could complete their swing, and the herd went rushing headlong for that western canyon and total destruction. *Christ, we'll never make it,* Dan thought in despair, raking his spurs. If the crazed creatures were not turned, they would plunge over the cliffs into the deep gorge of the Snake. And it would take some turning in the space available, with the storm-lashed beasts transformed into a thundering avalanche of beef, hurtling toward that chasm.

"Hit 'em hard!" Dan screamed uselessly. "Hit 'em and turn 'em."

Buffeted and half-blinded, Dan Ruylander bent his head into the pelting sleet and booted his bronc into full stride. Riding like a maniac, utterly reckless from sheer necessity, Dan raced abreast of the leaders and bore in perilously close to them, whipping his rope across their faces. In back of him galloped Kid Antrim and the rest of Rafter, along with the Oregon buckaroos, pressing in on the maddened steers. All riding like mad, flailing away at the brute heads with ropes and quirts, and finally firing sixguns in an effort to divert the cattle away from that precipice.

At last the point was turning slowly, bending away under the daring pressure of Dan Ruylander and the other riders, swerving gradually but surely into the north. The rimrock of the high bluff was close now, horrifyingly close in the blue-green flashes of lightning that etched the rain-soaked earth, and far below in its stony bed boiled the Snake River. But the herd was veering northward and parallel to the cliff, turning in an ever-sharpening arc.

Bearing in harder than ever upon that hurtling mass, Dan and his followers bent the torrent of beef back into the northeast and then the east, until the entire herd was curving, milling and slowing on the gusty plain. Its momentum fading and dying, the stampede was winding to an end in a dismal downpour of rain and hail. The storm was slackening abruptly, the worst of it already over, and the cattle wouldn't run any more tonight.

Reining up on his hard-blown gelding, Dan Ruylander turned to check his crew, feeling relief as he picked out one familiar face after another, drawn to the bone and burnished wet in the flicker of lightning. Big

Barnhorst, Rusty Fergus, old Jud Crater, and all the Triangle hands seemed to be present. *But where was Kid Antrim?* Someone else voiced that question, even as Dan put it into words, and somebody said: "The Kid went down back there. Under the herd."

Cold all over with a sinking nausea inside, Dan Ruylander said: "You saw him go under?"

"Yes, I saw it," Vern Winslett said, in calm tones. "His pony slipped or stepped in a hole or something. Antrim never had a chance."

"Like hell!" flared Rusty Fergus, insane with grief and hatred. "One of you scum shot the Kid's horse down. Winslett, I think—or maybe Fallon."

Hawk Fallon and Vern Winslett flung from their saddles, and Rusty Fergus stepped down to face them, a stark slender figure. Fallon said, "You lie, boy," and Winslett said, "Let me have him, Hawk."

"Back that up with guns," Fergus said, biting off the words. "Come on, the both of you. Start reaching, you sonsabitches!"

Dan Ruylander threw off and thrust in between them, gun in hand, and Garry Terrell was out of his saddle and pushing in from the other side, shaking his pistol at Fallon and Winslett.

"Hold it, boys," Dan said sharply. "There isn't going to be an gunplay here. Garry, keep your men in hand. And Rafter—we'll go back and look for the Kid."

"What's all the crying about?" Hawk Fallon demanded. "We lost two and now you've lost two. We had to take it, so you'll have to."

Leading their horses, the Wyoming men walked back over the chopped course of the stampede in the lessening rain and wind, searching the gouged and hoof-torn terrain.

There was scarcely enough left of Kid Antrim's boyish face and slim body to identify him, except for the bright blond hair on his crushed skull. But there was enough left of the trampled horse for them to find a bullethole in the carcass. It was murder again, just as it had been with Kiowa Kempter. Dan Ruylander turned away, sick with a stomach-wrenching sickness, but there was no time for that. He and Jud Crater had to restrain the Redhead and Barney by main force, from going directly after Triangle with their guns. Rusty Fergus was crying like a child, and the others kept blinking and swallowing in dry anguish.

Jud Crater wrapped a blanket around Kid Antrim's mutilated form, and big Barnhorst lifted it across his mount in front of the pommel. The smell of blood set the horse to pitching, but Barney pulled him down with his great strength. Dan borrowed Jud's tobacco plug and bit off a chew, his long arm around Rusty's quivering shoulders.

The score is even now, as Fallon said, Dan thought bitterly. *We lost the Injun and the Kid, and they lost Sowerby and Urbom. Anybody might be next. And if it keeps on, none of us will live to see Wyoming.*

"I'm going to kill 'em all, Dan," sobbed Rusty Fergus. "Every last goddamn one of 'em!"

"We'll get to them in time, Red," said Dan Ruylander somberly. "But you can't have 'em all, Rusty. I think Hawk Fallon's going to be mine."

Jud Crater stared across the glistening wet plain at the drifting stock. "It'll take all day tomorrow to gather the herd, Danny. And we better hire a couple of hands in Blackfoot, if we can. It's still a long ways home to the Sweetwater, son."

Twenty-Two

The day after the storm they rounded up the scattered cattle once more, and Dan Ruylander hired a pair of riders in town to augment the decimated crew. A discharged soldier named Rousch and a Mexican called Vaca were the replacements. These two, with the Sioux wrangler and the homestead boy Halley, gave the outfit four absolute neutrals. And thus far the Terrells and Smitty had maintained a middle course of neutrality—at least, on the surface. But Dan was still skeptical about Garry Terrell.

The Oregon men had tried to convert young Halley to the Triangle cause, but Hal had become too fond of Rusty Fergus and the dead Kid Antrim to forsake the Rafter side. When they buried the Kid that morning, tears had streamed down Halley's cheeks as well as Fergus's.

Four men dead since the drive started from the North Powder River of Oregon. Two Rafter men slain treacherously, and two Triangle hands killed in fair combat. Barney had told his mates about the underground fight with Pike Urbom, of course. Dan Ruylander thought the killings had stemmed from a natural instinctive enmity between the Oregon and Wyoming riders, rather than from any plan on the part of Garry Terrell. But there was no certainty in his belief, and no true foundation for it. If Owen Terrell had betrayed an old friend like Dirk Ruylander, it was quite possible his son would double-cross a new friend like Dan.

On the morning of departure from the camp outside of Blackfoot and the grave of Kid Antrim, Smitty's cookfire was crackling before dawn, and the bells of the cavvy chimed as the Indian wrangler brought in the horses. Breakfast over, the drive moved out along a grassy divide, with meadowlarks fluting sweetly, magpies scolding harshly, and sage-hens and chicks scampering before foraging gophers and prairie dogs. It was a beautiful summer morning, and Dan Ruylander felt a deep pang in his throat and breast, as he glanced back at the crude cross-marked burial place and thought of the gay laughing Kid cut down in the golden prime of his youth.

The grass on this section of the Oregon Trail had been eaten out to the roots by sheep, and Jud Crater advised taking Lander's Cutoff, which would afford better graze and shorten the distance from Fort Hall to South Pass by some sixty miles.

"Sheep!" said old Jud, spitting with a cowman's loathing for the wool-bearing animals. "One herder and two dogs can move three thousand sheep, and you need a dozen riders and a hundred horses to trail-drive that many cattle."

But on the Lander Road a plague of "Mormon Crickets" hit them, and Jud said: "It would've been better to follow the stinking sheep." These large locusts clouded the air and carpeted the earth, devouring everything that grew, stripping the vegetation clean and bare. They ate all the leaves off the cottonwoods and box elders, and ravished the chokecherry and buffalo-berry plants. It was impossible to cook or eat or sleep under this swarming visitation of insects, which left a raw barren waste wherever they landed and drove men and beasts to distraction. Until they finally reached a half-mile strip burned out by Indians, which freed them at last from the avaricious crickets.

With so many outside elements to contend with, there was no room for inner dissension and strife, but Rafter and Triangle still eyed each other with wary distrust and pent-up hatred. And there was murder in Hawk Fallon's yellow eyes every time he saw Dan Ruylander talking to Sue Terrell.

Garry Terrell kept his distance from Dan and the other Rafter hands. He was polite enough, even cordial, but always with a certain coolness and reserve and no more warm easy friendliness. *Sadie McLain sure poisoned him against me,* Dan decided, with some regret. *And Garry in turn soured his sister on me. Or maybe it's because they're plotting a deal to pull off before we hit Wyoming.*

"I still can't figure this Terrell, Jud," said Dan Ruylander, as they jogged along at the flank of the red herd. "You think he'll try anything?"

"If he does it'll come before we reach Rafter," said Jud Crater. "He's either hatching something, Dan, or that Sadie gal turned him against us."

Rusty Fergus, in his loneliness after Antrim's loss, had more or less adopted the Halley kid, and it was touching as well as amusing to observe the Redhead's fatherly interest in the hero-worshipping farm boy, who couldn't have been much younger than Rusty. They worked together whenever possible, and Hal was becoming a pretty fair hand under Rusty's tutelage. Hal tried to ride and walk, smile and talk and laugh like the Redhead. Occasionally Dan heard Rusty teaching Hal some of the range songs he had sung with Kid Antrim:

> *"Far away from his dear old Texas,*
> *We laid him down to rest;*
> *With his saddle for a pillow,*
> *And his sixgun on his chest."*

Soldier Rousch, a mild quiet man of medium size with a pleasant manner about him, was getting to be a comrade of Barnhorst, and thus the Oregon crew had lost out on two possible recruits. In return for which

169

they treated Halley and Rousch with insolent contempt, but were careful not to go far enough to arouse Rusty Fergus and big Barney.

August had blazed to an end when they skirted the southern shore of John Gray's Lake, with the Caribou Range rising in the north and the Rockies of the Great Divide looming closer and higher ahead of them. The eastern boundary of Idaho and the homeland of Wyoming were only twenty-odd miles away now.

After watering out and bedding down the stock, they bivouacked on the lakeshore, bathing and swimming in the cool clean water before supper. In the morning when the sun cleared the eastern crests, they were on the trail again and driving toward the border. It was a lovely land in golden-bright September, with rich grass, cold spring water and plentiful firewood. A veritable paradise after the lava-bed and cinder-cone country of middle Idaho.

They crossed Stump Creek, with its commercial salt works, and picked up some salt for the animals. They splashed through Boulder Creek and White Creek, and plodded on to make camp close below Targhee Ridge, which formed the boundary between Idaho and Wyoming Territorites at this point. "Over the hill is Wyoming," the Rafter riders told one another. "Ain't that something though?" jeered the Oregon men, exchanging satirical winks and grimaces. "I suppose we're really going to see something tomorrow. God's own favorite country at last!"

In these timbered foothills were deer and antelope. Deathly tired of beefs, beans and bacon, sourdough biscuits and Smitty's hash, some of the boys took their rifles into the woods and returned with game enough to provide venison and antelope steaks for several days.

Both men and animals had taken on a wild primitive aspect by this time, weathered dark and tough as rawhide from constant exposure to the elements, worn lean and fine and bone-hard from two months of trail-driving in the summer heat.

"I wonder where Sadie McLain will be waiting this time?" mused Dan Ruylander, puffing on his pipe and watching the moon rise over Targhee Ridge. "On the front porch at Rafter maybe."

"Rongis is the next settlement we hit," Jud Crater said. "She'll probably be on duty in John Signor's famous emporium."

"With Silk Coniff staked out somewhere with a rifle," Barnhorst added. "That Silk ain't going to give up until he's dead, Danny."

"Which he'll be damn sudden the next time he shows," declared Rusty Fergus, his red head gleaming in the firelight.

Mex Vaca and Soldier Rousch were out on first watch at the bed grounds, and young Halley was helping the Sioux wrangle the remuda this evening. On the other side of camp Triangle lounged at ease, with Hawk Fallon sprawled between Chill Cahoon and Vern Winslett. A short distance apart from them, Sue and Garry Terrell sat side by side against a wagon wheel. Smitty had gone to climb the ridge and get his first look in years at old Wyoming.

There was pure venom in the looks that passed between the two groups. With Wyoming so near, the tension and pressure were mounting even higher. The Oregon men seemed to expect Rafter to jump them and run off the herd. It was almost as if Terrell knew that the check he held was worthless. Rafter, on the other hand, was ever alert against a surprise attack by Triangle. Whatever Terrell's game might be, he would have to make his play before long now, or the Wyoming riders would be safe and secure in their own backyard.

Terrell couldn't have designs on the cattle, or he wouldn't have come this far east with the herd. But he might have ideas about wiping out Ruylander and the

Rafter crew. More and more Dan was coming to believe that Garry and Sue knew what had transpired between his father and their parents. An ungrounded hunch, but a strong one.

"We get held up much more we won't make fall roundup," Jud Crater grumbled. "Reckon we ain't going to make it anyway."

"Hellfire!" laughed Rusty Fergus. "I thought we was going to get a month's vacation with pay, at the end of this drive. Ain't you seen enough goddamn cows without going out on roundup the minute we hit home?"

"You young fellas can't stand the gaff," Jud said. "Old Dirk and me hunted buffalo all winter on the Staked Plains, and drove cattle up the trail all that next summer. We wasn't so young at the time neither."

"Never mind that ancient history, Jud," drawled Barnhorst. "Come a showdown, how you figure us four stack up against them four?"

"Pretty even, Barney," said Crater, after due consideration. "They lost their two strong boys, but they got their best gunhands left. Terrell and Fallon are real good, and Cahoon and Winslett are good enough. It shapes up a mite too even for comfort."

"The Injun wasn't so hot with a gun, but he could whale hell out of a half-dozen ordinary men with his bare hands," Barnhorst said thoughtfully. "The Kid was sharp with a Colt, of course. I ain't exactly greased lightning, but I reckon I can hold my own with Cahoon and Winslett. And the rest of you are better than me."

"I doubt if anybody can outdraw Fallon," said Crater. "The thing to do with Hawk is to outshoot him, if you can keep the range long enough. I might've done that once, and maybe Dan and Rusty could do it now. And I'd guess that Terrell's as fast as Fallon."

"To hell with this kind of talk," Dan Ruylander said, grinning to soften the sharpness of his words. "We'll do

172

all right—if it ever comes to that."

"Always have, Dan," agreed Jud Crater. "Reckon we always will."

Twenty-Three

In the gray morning fog after breakfast, the men were roping their horses out of the remuda when Rusty Fergus and Chill Cahoon got their lariats tangled up. Cursing and dropping the ropes, they flew at one another's throats like enraged wildcats and went down rolling and thrashing and tearing up the sod.

Hawk Fallon lunged in to reach for Fergus, but Barnhorst drove forward and shouldered the Hawk into a backward stagger. His spurs caught and tripped him, and Fallon sat down heavily, his hand flicking to his gun. It looked as if it was coming for sure now, but Garry Terrell rammed into Fallon and wrestled him flat on the turf, while Dan Ruylander ripped the entangled Fergus and Cahoon apart, and Jud Crater and others pinned them to the ground.

It was broken up almost as quickly as it started, but everyone there felt it was just another postponement of the inevitable. This had been brewing since early June, and it was bound to break out and embroil them all before long. There was too much hate and fury on both sides to be contained for any length of time. Each crew had two deaths to avenge, and they wouldn't rest until it was done. Or until bullets checked them.

The roping out and saddling up continued, and the camp resembled a rodeo arena as the broncs bucked and fought under the cold damp leather. Young Halley was pitched off into a clump of buckbrush, and Triangle howled with malicious merriment until silenced by Terrell. When Rousch's horse bumped into Winslett's Vern was about to quirt the Soldier, but the high rawboned presence of Barnhorst restrained him. The wagons creaked out toward the ridge, and the Sioux took his cavvy after them. Dan Ruylander cut out the lead steers, and the herd was on the road again.

The trail wound over the rough forested hump of Targhee into the ruddy glare of the rising sun, and down the eastern slope to the soil of Wyoming. The herd entered the territory at the upper-end of Star Valley, with the Salt River Range standing on the east. Far to the north towered the sharp snow-frosted rock pinnacles of the Grand Tetons, soaring in fabulous beauty like mountains in a fairy tale.

They made their first homeland camp on Salt River, and followed it upstream to the south the next day.

After leaving the Salt, they forded Smith's Fork and drove on through a broken pass between Wyoming Peak and Mount Thompson to the LaBarge Meadows. Excellent camp sites were located every night, and with richer graze and easier going the cattle, horses and men were all improving in condition and appearance. On Middle Piney Creek, after forewarning Sue Terrell, all hands bathed, shaved and sheared one another's hair, the close-cropped results laughable in most instances.

And still Triangle was riding it out, holding their hands and biding their time, waiting for some reason that Dan Ruylander could not fathom. Every day brought them fifteen or more miles nearer to South Pass, the Sweetwater, and the home spread of Rafter.

Green River was crossed with September on the wane, and the drive rolled due east on Alkali Creek to the Muddy, and then southeast to Big Sandy Creek. Here they encountered some of the poorest country in all

Wyoming. The streams ran low and dry; feed and water and firewood were extremely scarce. Smitty had to use cow chips for fuel, as he had in some of the volcanic wastes of Idaho.

Down the Big Squaw they drifted and pushed the red-and-white cattle, eating dust and grit all day in the ceaseless winds of Wyoming. *Git along, you dogies, git along cow critters, For this is Wyoming and you're almost home.*

On to Little Sandy Creek and east toward the magnificent ramparts of the Continental Divide, with the Wind River Mountains jutting high on the north. Then the mountain passage was before them, and beyond the great barrier lay the plains of the Sweetwater and home.

South Pass, known to the old mountain men and fur traders, the westbound emigrants, Mormons and gold-seekers, the Overland Stage Line and the Pony Express, crossed the Divide at about 7,500 feet, a surprisingly easy and gradual climb and descent.

The summer was spent and autumn reigned in this high country, with crickets chirping and aspens rippling bronze and golden against the somber dark green of lodgepole pine and Douglas fir. There were fewer flies and insects and far less heat at this altitude, and grass and water and wood for fuel were available in abundance. The mountain air was fresh, clean and invigorating, as sparkling and heady as good old brandy.

But the riders were strangely subdued and solemn, in spite of the bright winelike atmosphere, for there was an aura of ages-old mystery and tradition in South Pass. Dan Ruylander felt it keenly, and in his mind he visualized ghostly processions of long-dead men and women who had passed this way, heading for Oregon or California or Salt Lake City. A new life in new country, and death that came far away from birthplaces and homes.

"It'll probably come in Rongis, Danny," said old Jud Crater, as they toiled slowly along the highland passage with the strung-out herd. "They must know about that place. No law there whatever, and far enough away from Rafter to be safe."

"I've got the same feeling, Jud," said Dan Ruylander, shifting wearily in the hot damp saddle. "They figure we'll let down a little, with the drive almost over. Rongis is the place all right."

"If it comes to shooting, son," Jud murmured. "You want me to take Terrell?"

Dan shook his tawny head. "Not necessarily, Jud. Just have to take 'em as they come, I guess. I want Fallon myself, but there's no telling how it'll turn out."

"You've done a great job, boy. Wanted to tell you, in case something goes wrong—before we get home."

Dan grinned at him. "Have to ask you what you asked me once, the night before we started the drive. What the hell kind of talk is that?"

"I ain't fixing to die," Jud Crater said, with a sheepish grimace. "But I got a feeling lately. It ain't right for these kids to go under, and leave an old coot like me on top of the ground."

"Never thought I'd see you soften up and start cracking," Dan Ruylander said, with forced sternness.

"Who the hell is?" demanded Crater. "That'll be the goddamn day when I soften and crack! Don't fret about this old rooster, son. I'll outlast the whole pack of you young sprouts, by jeezus!"

"That's better, Jud," said Dan, smiling with pleasure. "More like yourself. You're too damn ornery mean to die anyway."

"You said something, kid," grinned Jud Crater. "I'm pure poison. Sometimes I almost scare hell out of myself.''

They filed the stock down the narrow winding road on the eastern slopes of the Divide, and Dan Ruylander missed Kiowa Kempter and Kid Antrim more than ever as they neared the home range. The Injun and the Kid had loved Wyoming and Rafter as much as Dan did, and they'd been like members of the family, more like brothers or friends than hired hands.

Picking up the headwaters of Lander Creek on the mountainside, they followed it down and out of South Pass to the upper fork of the Sweetwater River. Now they were really in the home stretch at the end of September, with the great buffalo plains sweeping and rolling eastward before them. A country of vast bronzed distances, with mountains piled to the north and south of these broad central lowlands.

Another day's drive to Rongis, and then three more days to Rafter. About sixty miles from this camp site at the eastern foot of the Divide to the home ranch on the Sweetwater. Dan was eager and impatient to get there now, and to see his father and brother Hud and sister Judith. Progress in the next four days would seem maddeningly slow, with the herd a massive and unwieldy burden to move over the golden brown prairies.

What if they don't start anything in Rongis? pondered Dan Ruylander, over his tin supper plate. How am I going to handle the pay-off at Rafter, dispose of the Terrells and Triangle, say goodbye and shut Sue out of my life forever? But he knew Hawk Fallon would start something, if Garry Terrell did not. There'd be a gunfight with the Hawk, no matter what else happened. This would be the end of the trail for one—or both—of them. The West was no longer large enough to hold both Dan Ruylander and Hawk Fallon. And once the Hawk opened up, the others would pitch in.

Dan couldn't foresee any way out of the ultimate showdown, a final free-for-all gun battle.

He should have been marrying Sue Terrell, but there were too many barriers between them: A thirty-year feud, a stolen herd of cattle, and a worthless check. But Dan Ruylander had the cash in his money belt to pay for the stock. When they reached Rafter—if they ever did—he could prevail upon Dirk to buy the herd. But the long-delayed outburst was apt to occur in Rongis, some forty-five miles this side of the home spread.

That night the plains were flooded with brilliant moonlight, and Dan Ruylander walked away from the campfire to lean upon a boulder at the base of an erosion butte. His heart went up and his throat filled tautly, when he saw Sue Terrell striding in his direction. Dan had tried to will her into following him this evening, and it almost seemed that he had succeeded. She came straight to his side, but there was still an aloofness about her. Sue's face was drawn from the hardships of the trail, and the bone structure had an even greater sculptural beauty, Dan thought.

"Tomorrow night we'll be in a town called Rongis?" she said, and went on as he nodded in affirmation. "I'm afraid, Dan. Something's going to happen there. And it's not good."

"What, Sue? You mean Hawk Fallon?"

Her dark head dipped. "He intends to kill you, Dan."

Ruylander smiled thinly. "Well, he can try. Is Garry going to side with him?"

"I don't know, Dan," she murmured brokenly. "I don't know what Garry will do any more. That McLain woman has done something to him. He isn't the same man at all."

"And that has come between us, Sue?"

"Oh, Dan," she sighed. "There's a lot more than

that between us.''

Dan Ruylander wanted to break down then and give her the whole story, and find out how much of it she and Garry already knew, but he could not do it. He couldn't trust anyone named Terrell too far. He said: "What do you mean, Sue?''

"I don't know. It doesn't make any difference, I guess.''

"Wish I knew how Garry felt—about everything.''

Sue Terrell looked up at him. "I won't let Garry shoot you, Dan. But I—I can't stop Hawk Fallon.''

"I'll stop him, Sue,'' said Ruylander, with quiet grimness. "But I'd hate to use a gun on your brother.''

There was an interlude of silence, as their eyes searched the limitless expanse of jeweled skies and silvered land. Dan wanted to haul her into his arms, by force if necessary, but his pride wouldn't permit the attempt. Since the rebuff at old Fort Hall, he hadn't made a single advance toward her.

"Well, I'd better go back,'' Sue Terrell said finally, a tremor shaking her lithe body. "It—it's cold out here.''

"I could keep you warm, Sue.''

"No—not any more, Dan. The coldness is inside. But I love this country of yours. The plains stretching like a brown ocean, and the mountains reaching into the clouds. But I must go, Danny.''

His smile was sorrowful. "Glad you came out, Sue, even if you won't stay. Maybe, when we get to Rafter . . .''

"Maybe,'' whispered the girl. "If we do get there, Dan.'' She whirled abruptly, almost running across the moonlit prairie toward the encampment, and Ruylander was left more bewildered than before.

On watch later that night, standing the graveyard shift from two to four o'clock, Dan Ruylander wondered if this morning's sunrise would be his last. It would be ironic to die this near to home, after surviving all the dangers and ordeals of the past four months, with death brushing by close enough to touch so many times. But that's the way things happened. Life, as well as death, was filled with ironies.

Dan wasn't too afraid. A little fear, a dread of dying, was only natural. He was anxious to get it over and done with. It had been waiting, hanging fire, for an unbearably long time. By this hour tomorrow night it should be finished, one way or another. He'd either be with Kiowa and the Kid, or still among the living.

Dan Ruylander wanted to look at Hawk Fallon over a gun barrel, but he didn't like to think of lifting a gun against Garry Terrell.

Twenty-Four

The next afternoon brought Rongis into view, its rude buildings scattered on the plain as if by a careless giant hand, the Sweetwater flowing past on the south with the Antelope Hills moulded gauntly along the southern background. On the river flats outside of the sprawling settlement was a fenced-in holding ground, and they pointed the herd in that direction as a motley crowd gathered to watch them drive in through billowing dust clouds.

This was John Signor's town, and he had given it his name—spelled backwards and pronounced Rongee. He owned this stockyard on the southern outskirts, along with the stage station and primitive hotel at the center of the community, and the notorious roadhouse on the eastern rim. There was no law here but John Signor's law, and Rongis was a rendezvous and hideout for bandits, rustlers, fugitives, and derelicts. But they never stole anything from John Signor, nor any cattle from his spacious pen. The place was wide open, a sinkhole of evil and vice, yet John Signor himself was regarded as an honest and honorable man. He helped many deserving unfortunates, and rendered swift justice to many vicious criminals. He never turned anyone away hungry or thirsty, or wanting for care and shelter.

"John Signor built himself a little hell here, and he presides over it like a saint," Jud Crater declared, as they punched the stock through the wide gate of the holding ground. "He's as much of a gentleman as old Granville Stuart of Montana, who came west from a first family of Virginia, and Gran always stops to see John when he's down this way. Among Signor's friends are the best and the worst people of Wyoming. Take Dirk Ruylander to represent the best, and Cattle Kate Maxwell the worst, for instance. John Signor would throw out the Governor if he misbehaved, and he'd serve the poorest two-bit thief unhung if he acted decent. That's democracy, by God, as you seldom see it!"

The cattle in the yard and the horse herd in a huge corral, the wagons parked and saddle gear slung to dry, the trail crew took their warbags out of the Schuttler and straggled in toward town. The unpainted weatherbeaten buildings, some of them with sod or thatched roofs, looked as if they had grown up raw from the reddish-brown earth. The only two-storied structures were the shoddy hotel and the long rambling roadhouse. The single street had a few saloons and stores, a barber shop, a blacksmith's forge, a pool hall, restaurant, and harness-maker's establishment. The stage depot stood opposite the hotel, and was even more decrepit. The outlying houses were strewn about at random.

Rongis held many assorted memories for Dan Ruylander, both bitter and sweet. Here he had fallen in and out of love, gone on his first drunk, fought his first gun battle, and had his first woman. A lot of his growing up had been done in this sordid settlement, and tonight it might be the scene of his last gunfight—and his death. But Dan refused to dwell on that morbid matter. Rafter often came here to celebrate holidays and the end of roundups, and at John Signor's bar Dan had emptied many a bottle with his present companions and others, including Kiowa Kempter and Kid Antrim.

Now Sue and Garry Terrell entered the hotel, while their Triangle men rushed the barber shop. "We better get rooms and clean up here," Dan Ruylander said, leading his crew into the lobby. "Never get into that barber's." Vaca and the Sioux said they preferred to sleep outside, so Dan hired three rooms, sharing one with Jud, while Barnhorst and Rousch occupied another, and Rusty Fergus and Halley took the third. They carried up their own water to bathe, shave, and then change into clean clothing. These operations completed and a drink under their belts, they felt almost civilized again.

Descending to gather on the crumbling gallery of the hotel, they started walking out toward John Signor's far- and ill-famed roadhouse, and Dan saw the Mexican and Indian hunched at the lunch counter as they passed the restaurant. Behind them the sun was setting beyond the western heights, painting the clouds with fiery colors as twilight spread, calm and peaceful, on the autumn land.

Dan spoke to Halley and Rousch: "If any trouble starts, you two boys keep out of it. No fight of yours. It's between us four and the four from Oregon."

"What's between the two outfits anyway, Dan?" asked Rousch.

"We just go against each other's grain, Soldier," said Dan Ruylander. "This has been building up all summer."

"If they jump Rusty I'm getting into it," Halley said.

"Not as long as it's a fair fight, son," said Rousch, with gentle tact. "These Wyoming men won't need any help from us."

Fergus nodded his red head firmly. "That's right, Hal. You stay the hell clear of it. They're real tough sonsabitches."

"But you been showing me how to use a gun, Rusty."

"You're doing okay, too, Hal," said Fergus soberly. "But you ain't quite ready for professionals yet."

In the roadhouse, John Signor came forward to greet them and shake hands with them, and Dan Ruylander introduced the new riders to him.

"The Injunand the Kid?" asked Signor softly.

"Gone, John. They got it on the trail back."

"I'm sorry to hear that," Signor said, with simple sincerity. "I was fond of those two boys. And five or six of my girls are going to be all broken up, I'm afraid. Your pleasure now, gentlemen? The first three rounds are on me tonight."

They drank at the long bar, the place quiet and almost deserted at this early hour, and discussed various topics with the proprietor. Dan inquired after his family and Rafter, and Signor said they were all well and everything was fine at the ranch, as far as he knew. But Dirk was anxiously awaiting their return. Signor told them that President Garfield had finally died on September 19th, and an obscure Vermonter named Chester A. Arthur was in the White House.

Signor in turned listened with grave interest and intelligent comments, as they told him something of Oregon and their journey out and back. He was a tall, distinguished-looking man of quiet assurance and indeterminate age, with a pleasantly ugly face carved by deep somber lines. His wavy hair was graying, but his eyes were young, clear and piercing, and his slow smile had a singular charm.

When questioned about Silk Coniff, he said: "I haven't had the dubious pleasure of seeing that suave scoundrel since last winter or early spring. I am gratified to hear that his illustrious associates, Haydock and Klugstad, came to a fitting end in Baker City. My sole regret is that Coniff isn't buried out there with them."

"There may be trouble here tonight, John," said Dan Ruylander.

"You know I detest trouble, Dan," said John Signor mildly. "But tell me about it anyway."

Ruylander sketched the situation briefly for him, and Signor nodded with solemn understanding. "But can't you have it elsewhere, Danny?" he asked. "This is supposed to be a palace of pleasure, as you may recall. It doesn't really require a blood bath this evening."

"We'll try not to have it in here, John," said Dan. "But I thought I'd tell you about it in advance."

"I appreciate that, Danny. Are you gentlemen going to dine here? I can offer you some truly delicious baked ham, a fare that you might have missed on the trail."

"Sounds mighty good to me, John," said Jud Crater, and the others were in agreement.

Signor indicated a table for them, and smiled warmly at Crater. "I guess, Jud, you're going to live forever, you ancient reprobate."

"Hope not," Crater said, in his gravel voice. "But if I live through tonight, John, maybe I will last a few more years."

"Let me take one of your sawed-off shotguns, John," requested big Barnhorst. "With that maybe I can control things in here, and force the fight outsie—if there is any."

184

"Not a bad suggestion, Barney," said John Signor, reaching under the bar and bringing up a stubby double-barrled shotgun. "You can sit against the wall and keep this under the table. It's a powerful persuader indeed."

The roadhouse was bare and crudely furnished, its bar and tables of rough planks, but the food and liquor were of the finest quality. They finished eating and lingered comfortably over coffee, brandy, and long cigars, as the place began to fill up for the evening. A small orchestra began to play, as the bright-gowned percentage girls came into circulation. Bonny and Estrella came over to inquire for Kid Antrim and Kiowa Kempter, and fled the room at once on hearing the bad news. The gambling layouts began to hum within deepening rings of humanity, and another night was underway at John Signor's.

Sue Terrell, lovely in a simple blue dress, came in on her brother's arm, the girl nodding at Rafter and Garry smiling and saluting with a flash of his old-time cheer and warmth. They took a table for two across the way and ordered drinks, evidently having had supper in town, and Garry had another round of brandy sent to the Rafter party.

A few minutes later Hawk Fallon entered in his easy swagger, flanked by dapper Vern Winslett and the dark, menacing Chill Cahoon. They were freshly barbered and slicked up, each wearing two guns tonight, and Dan Ruylander knew it was coming now. The Triangle riders sat down at a table near the Terrells and surveyed the scene with careless contempt. Hawk Fallon, with his dark auburn hair and fierce amber eyes, was handsome in a bold predatory fashion this evening. And the stage was set for violence and tragedy.

Two hours later the revelry was in full swing. Dan Ruylander had accepted Garry Terrell's invitation to join him and his sister, and the two men were smoking and sipping drinks while Sue watched the dance floor, on which Rusty Fergus and young Halley cavorted with partners from time to time. Barnhorst was still in his original place, rangy broad shoulders against the wall and the sawed-off Greener under the table. Bonny and Estrella had reappeared to join Barney, drinking and refusing all offers to dance.

Old Jud Crater and Hawk Fallon stood well apart and watchful of one another at the long plank bar, behind which John Signor and two bartenders were at work. Soldier Rousch wandered idly among the gaming tables, pausing to watch the play here and there. Vaca and the Sioux were outside somewhere with a bottle the Mexican had smuggled to the Indian, and Smitty was no doubt standing unnecessary guard over the wagons and stock on the river flats.

At a table near the dancehall end of the great smoke-hazed room, Vern Winslett and Chill Cahoon flirted with a pair of Signor's percentage girls and watched Rusty Fergus with cold steady eyes. Barney in turn had them under close surveillance, while Crater and Fallon covered the entire assemblage from the bar, and Ruylander and Terrell observed every detail from their table.

Garry Terrell was affable, friendly and winning, but Dan didn't know how deep and sincere it went. Apparently Sadie McLain had not arrived in Rongis. Sue was withdrawn and silent, the strain showing in her blue eyes and finely drawn features. Dan Ruylander couldn't look at her without wanting her, so he kept his gray glance diverted most of the time. There was too much else to watch anyway. Desire had no place in the pattern of this night.

"Dan, I'm sorry for the way I was on the road," Garry Terrell admitted finally. "I listened to a woman when I knew damn well she was lying. But it's all over now, Danny. She must have made her choice in Blackfoot. Sadie McLain stayed back there—with Silk Coniff, I imagine. Instead of coming to meet me here."

"Then you're lucky, Garry," drawled Ruylander. "And we're friends again?"

"I hope so, Dan. If you can forgive me."

"What if Fallon makes his move—tonight?"

"I'll try and stop him. But I'm not promising I can. Hawk's waited longer than I ever expected him to, Dan."

Dan Ruylander sighed. "Wouldn't mind him so much, if the others would stay out of it."

"I know, Danny," said Terrell, a frown fretting his chiseled face and narrowing his brown eyes. "But they'll follow the Hawk, I'm afraid. They're his men more than mine."

"Well, let 'em come," Dan murmured. "I'd like to get it settled."

Rusty Fergus was waltzing with a flamboyant charmer of mixed Latin ancestry, gliding along by the far wall, when someone tapped his shoulder. Thinking it was Halley, since they'd been cutting in on each other right along, Fergus let go of his partner and turned with a grin. But it was Chill Cahoon, poised to strike, and his wicked punch caught Fergus flush on the chin, snapping his red head back.

Reeling backward against a window, Rusty's boots struck the low sill and tripped him, shoulders and head crashing through the glass. He landed outside in the dirt, flat on his back with a ringing head and the breath beaten from his lungs, bright shards scattered about him.

Fergus threshed into a desperate roll and clawed out his Colt, just as Cahoon's gun roared down from the broken window, the bullet ripping up dust from the spot Rusty had barely vacated. Chill Cahoon was framed in the lamplit window, throwing down from the recoil, when Rusty Fergus lifted his gun from a prone position and let go a quick blast. Cahoon's pistol blared aimlessly at the sky, as he jerked back and spun, toppling out of sight.

Springing swiftly upright Rusty Fergus reached the glass-sharded windowsill and saw Cahoon squirming on the waxed hardwood with his carmined left hand clutching his smashed right shoulder. Before Fergus could slam another slug into the man, flame leaped at his face from Vern Winslett's hand, and Rusty ducked and dropped under a slashing shower of glass and wood-splinters.

Inside screaming women and cursing men scattered hastily, leaving the dance floor vacant except for Chill Cahoon's writhing body and the trim elegant Vern Winslett. Young Halley came running at him, dragging awkwardly at his gun handle, and Winslett smiled as he leveled off at the Idaho boy. But Barnhorst's voice lashed out through the swirling smoke, before Winslett could trigger: "This way, Vern! Drop that iron or I'll blow you apart!" And Barney was towering there at the edge of the floor, with the double-barreled shotgun lined on the Oregon man. "Hold it, you slick bastard!"

Vern Winslett swiveled smoothly to swing his pistol to bear on Barnhorst, but Barney held low and let go with both barrels. The bellowing blast swelled against walls and ceiling and shook the whole building, with lamplight flickering tall and the smoke wreaths shredded ragged. The double charge of buckshot smashed Winslett's legs from under him, and flung him rolling on the floor like a bloody tattered bundle of cloth. He sprawled there like a corpse, but Barney knew that only his legs were shattered. And Chill Cahoon was unconscious now from the shock and pain of his wounded shoulder. Both down and out of the fight, but they'd live and recover—if old Doc Saulteras was sober enough to attend them.

The fiery thatch of Rusty Fergus appeared again in the ruined window, and Barnhorst reached out a mighty hand to hoist the Redhead in over the sill. "Getting real careless, Rusty," he said. "Letting yourself get clipped like that."

Hawk Fallon had left the bar to stride toward the Terrell table, saying: "All right, Ruylander, on your feet. It's our turn now."

Dan and Garry Terrell rose slowly together, and Garry said: "There's been enough shooting, Hawk."

Fallon glared at him, outraged and incredulous. "What the hell's eating you, Garry? You going to let 'em wipe us out without lifting a finger? Your goddamn crew's gone now. Next they'll take the herd and your sister, and leave you dead in some gully, for chrisake!"

"I don't think so, Hawk," said Terrell calmly. "And don't start reaching, because Jud's got a gun on you."

"You're covered, Hawk," said old Jud Crater, his Colt lined steadily on Fallon's back. "Better take a walk, boy."

Hawk Fallon shrugged and stared at Ruylander. "I'll be waiting at the hotel, Wyoming."

"You won't have to wait long," Dan said, and watched Fallon walk out the door with lazy insolent arrogance.

Sue Terrell, pale under the tan, bowed her lustrous dark head into white-knuckled hands, and Dan Ruylander said: "Garry, you'd better take Sue to her room. We'll tend to the wounded." Terrell nodded and led his sister outside.

John Signor was there, speaking evenly: "Get a wagon, Dan, and take those boys to the doctor's. Saulteras wasn't drunk the last I knew."

Barnhorst handed him the shotgun. "Sorry, John. It

189

happened too fast."

"You did as well as any man could have, Barney," said Signor. "It could have been a whole lot worse here." He ordered someone to bring a wagon to the front door, while Barney and Jud took Rousch and Halley to help carry the wounded men out.

Rusty Fergus paused and handed Ruylander a Colt. "One of Winslett's, Dan. You might need the extra shots."

"Thanks, Red." Dan checked the weapon and thrust it under his waistband, and they trailed their comrades outside to load the unconscious Cahoon and Winslett onto a flat wagon-bed.

Jud Crater took the reins and climbed to the seat, with Rusty Fergus mounting to sit beside him. Dan handed Soldier Rousch some money and said: "You and Hal go back in and enjoy yourselves." Then he climbed on back of the vehicle. "I'll ride part way in, Jud." Barnhorst came out of the barroom with a bottle in his hand, and swung up beside Dan as Crater started the horses.

"I get off when you do, Danny," said Rusty Fergus.

"No, Redhead," said Ruylander, drinking from Barney's bottle. "This is for Fallon and me alone."

"What if Terrell sides with the Hawk?" asked Fergus.

"He won't. Garry's all right now."

Jud Crater spat aside. "Don't be too damn sure, Danny. One of us will go with you."

"I said no, Jud," insisted Dan Ruylander; with soft emphasis. "Fallon's been mine from the beginning."

"Don't get too close to him, son. Make him shoot from away." Jud Crater reined up, after making the turn toward Doc Saulteras's house on the north side, and Dan saw the Wind River Range and the Owl Creek Mountains jagged against the starlit nothern heavens.

Dropping lightly from the wagon, Dan raised an easy hand. "I'll be seeing you, boys. Save me some of that whiskey, Barney."

Twenty-Five

But Dan Ruylander did not feel as jaunty and confident as he had sounded, when he started his lone walk in toward the faint twinkling light at the center of Rongis. It was coming at last, and there was no alternative. It had to be done, and Dan had to do it himself. He walked with easy swinging strides, grateful that his muscles were loose and responsive, a big rangy shape in the shadow-scarred moonlight.

Ahead of him Sue and Garry Terrell had nearly reached the Continental House, an absurd name for that ramshackle trap of a frontier hotel, and the tall black-garbed form of Hawk Fallon appeared beside them. They halted to talk there, and Dan thought: *Maybe Garry will throw in with him after all. How the hell do I know? And if he does, I'm dead.* But Dan wouldn't turn back now, and he couldn't wait for the boys to come in. It was time Dan Ruylander did some fighting for himself and Rafter.

There was fear in him, but Dan thought it normal. No man wants to die at twenty-four—or any other age, for that matter. His stomach felt as queasy as it did after a drunk, and his heart fluttered in panic. His spinal column was chilled, and his leg muscles twitched as he walked. Dan Ruylander was frankly afraid, but he could control and master the dread. There was enough fire and hatred and fury inside to melt the icy clamp of fear. This was going to be tough. He'd never have to face anything much harder. But Dan was ready and willing, eager after the prolonged delay.

Time seemed to stand still and space remain static, as his boots crunched onward in steady rhythm, spurning moonlit crystals and shadow-blackened soil. When Dan was about fifty yards away, Hawk Fallon left the Terrells and moved out into the middle of the wide street, pacing forward with elastic grace to meet his opponent.

Better make him shoot long, Dan thought. *That way it won't matter so much, if he beats me on the draw. Give your man the first shot, if you have to, Jud and Dirk always said, but get your own first one home sure and solid.*

Sue Terrell suddenly broke away from her brother, and ran up the creaking steps into the hotel, and Dan Ruylander thought she must know that Garry was going to back Fallon's play, and she could not bear to watch it. Garry Terrell stood watching from the cracked sidewalk, his tailored coat brushed back to clear the holstered gun. He could have stopped the Hawk now, if he wanted to. Instead Garry was waiting to see the duel, and apparently ready to cut down on Dan if Hawk Fallon failed to kill him.

Dan Ruylander was in a trap, in so deep that his only chance was to shoot his way out. And against two men that was a very thin chance.

At about thirty yards, Dan stopped and called: "Let's have it, Hawk."

"Afraid to come in closer, Wyoming?" jeered Fallon, hesitating with mockery on his proud features. "Come on, you sonofabitch!"

"This too long a range for you?" Ruylander inquired.

"It don't matter to me," Hawk Fallon said, with that supreme assurance of his. "Man, I've waited a long time for this!''

Garry Terrell was still there at Dan's left and a bit behind Fallon, motionless as a tall statue in the light-filtered shadows.

"And you've come a long way to die, Hawk," said Dan.

Fallon's hand whipped, at that, and Dan tried to match his flowing speed and could not. The Hawk's muzzle flared with a bright orange roar in the dimness, and Dan Ruylander felt the searing suction of lead on his left cheek, as his own Colt cleared and lifted, his thumb working the hammer as the barrel came into line. Fallon was hit and jarred backward, and Dan knew he had the first one in there good and solid. But the Hawk was still on his feet and firing again, this shot slanting low and slashing dirt across Dan's boots.

Pulling down from the kickup, Dan Ruylander cut loose another slug, the flame lancing out and the gun jolting his wrist up, and dust spurting from the dark cloth on Hawk Fallon's chest. The wallop of the .44 smashed Fallon back on his heels and unhinged his knees. Fighting for balance, Hawk lunged forward on spraddled legs, stumbled and fell on all fours. His hat came off and his head sagged, but the Hawk was still straining to push himself up and raise his gunhand.

With a grunting heave Hawk Fallon came half erect and his pistol exploded without aim, the shot so wild that Dan didn't hear its passage. Throwing down once more, Dan Ruylander blasted another bullet home, and Fallon lurched backward into a twisting sprawl. With disjointed limbs flailing up dirt, he rolled and came up again, yellow eyes flaring madly in his agonized face, and Dan was reminded of a mountain lion he had seen one time, shot to pieces but still snarling and refusing to die.

But Hawk Fallon was dying on his feet now, the gun

in his hand too heavy to raise. His last shot raked up dust midway between them, and Dan was leveling off to fire again when he saw it wouldn't be necessary. Fallon collapsed all at once, pitching sidewise and rolling over onto his shoulderblades to lie spread-limbed, slack and lifeless in the deep churned gravel of the street. Dan Ruylander stalked up and stood over him for a moment, and then wheeled toward Terrell on the slat sidewalk.

"Well, Garry? You coming in or staying out?"

Terrell glanced at the smoking gun in Dan's hand. "Are you calling me, Danny?"

Ruylander holstered the Colt. "Come on. You've got nothing more to wait for."

"You want to fight me, Dan?"

"No, goddamn it! But I want to know where you stand, Garry."

"Not against you, Dan," said Garry Terrell. Then his hand swept into motion, as his face changed abruptly, and Dan knew he'd been tricked. But Terrell's eyes were staring beyond Dan, as he cried, "Look out behind you!"

In the same instant, the familiar mocking tones of Silk Coniff floated across the broad avenue: "Turn around and take your medicine, friend Dan."

Dan Ruylander drew and came around shooting, even as Coniff's pistol blazed at him, and the muzzle flames met and merged blindlingly. Dan felt the scorch of a near miss on his left elbow, and saw his own shot beat Silk back upon a hitch-rail in front of the stage depot, and knew how lucky he had been with that one.

Propped and crumpling there, Silk Coniff kept on firing, his gun flashing and beating up echoes along the empty street, and Dan felt the close hot breath of death all about him as he emptied his own .44 and ripped the borrowed Colt out of his belt. Opening up from a balanced crouch, Dan Ruylander hammered his lead into those torchlike flares and the street was streaked with lightning. But the hard-hit Silk was missing, while Dan was scoring steadily.

Buckling and shuddering against the rack, Silk Coniff finally broke down at the knees and waist, taking one lunging stride forward and plunging headlong with his face in the dirt. Dan Ruylander turned and walked away on numb legs, the concussions still dinning in his brain and the taste of powder making him gag, as the street began to swarm with curious excited people. Garry Terrell came out to meet him, saying:

"You all right, Danny? You're really hell with a sixgun, boy."

Dan wagged his head and spat from a dry mouth. "God, but they died hard. Both of them."

"They sure took a lot of killing, Dan," agreed Terrell, as they climbed the rickety stairs and went into the dim-lighted lobby. "I would have taken a shot at Coniff, but you were in between us."

"They were both mine, Garry," said Dan Ruylander. "Thank God it's finished."

"You need a drink, Danny. And I could use one too."

"Upstairs in the room. I don't want people around."

In Dan's room he sank down on the edge of the bed to punch out empty brass and reload the two guns, while Garry Terrell poured the drinks. Dan said, "Glad I didn't have to go against you, Garry."

Terrell grinned. "You're not as glad about that as I am!"

"This won't make you happy though," Dan Ruylander said slowly. "That check I gave you is no good."

"That's all right, Dan," said Terrell calmly. "I was going to tear it up anyway."

Dan stared at him. "What the hell do you mean by

that?"

"The herd's yours, Dan. I wasn't planning on taking any payment for it. If you hadn't come out after it, I'd have driven it east myself."

"I don't get it, Garry," said Dan wonderingly.

Terrell splashed out another round of whiskey. "My father willed those cattle to Rafter," he said quietly. "When he was dying, Dan, he told us what he had done to your dad in old Fort Laramie, back in 1851. It preyed on his mind all the rest of his life. He was never a happy man, and Mother wasn't happy either. Although they were fine parents to Sue and me. Dad made me promise to deliver a herd—or the cash value of one—to Dirk Ruylander of Rafter. So that's what we're doing, Danny."

"But we were going to steal the stock."

Terrell smiled. "Don't blame you a damn bit. Only it isn't necessary in this case, Dan. I'm sorry about the men who died. Two of yours and three of mine. But they didn't die fighting for the herd. They were killed fighting one another. There was bad blood between them from the start."

"Well, I'll be goddamned," Dan drawled, shaking his bronze head.

"Dad killed himself—after Mother died," Garry Terrell went on. "We tried to keep it quiet, but that's what happened. After Fort Laramie he lived with guilt and shame, and when Mother went he couldn't face it alone, I guess."

Someone rapped on the door, and Terrell opened it to admit his sister. Dan stood up and Sue ran forward into his arms, sobbing in quiet relief and thanksgiving as he held her with gentle firmness. Garry lit a cigar and stood by with glass in hand, regarding them with approval and satisfaction.

After an interval Sue lifted her wet blue eyes and

gazed at Dan Ruylander's face, as if to memorize every detail forever. The lean strong-boned features, polished a deep ruddy brown from sun and wind, and grimed now with powdersmoke. The eyes gray and clear, the mouth broadly gentle and handsome under the proud nose, and the fine head streaked sunnily in the lamplight.

"Garry told you, Dan? About everything?" Sue Terrell asked, and he inclined his tawny head. "But what were you going to do about me—if it hadn't turned out this way?"

"I don't rightly know, Sue." Ruylander frowned thoughtfully. "Steal you maybe, along with the cattle."

"We should have told you before, I guess."

"Might've eased my mind and conscience some. But it don't hurt a man to suffer things out."

"Yes, Dan. You're more of a man that you were four months ago. And you always were man enough."

"Just so I'm man enough for you, Sue," said Dan gravely.

She laughed softly. "You're all that and more, Danny. All the way down the trail."

"Think you'd like to live in Wyoming, Sue?"

"Anywhere you are, Dan," said Sue Terrell.

"Be kind of lonesome for me back in Oregon," mused Garry Terrell. "But maybe I can find a good wife for myself, once I get rid of my nagging overbearing sister. I'll be indebted to you, Dan, if you ever do take her off my hands."

Dan Ruylander smiled. "I'll tear up the check on that deal, Garry. I'll do it for you, for nothing at all."

"Three more days to Rafter," said Garry thoughtfully. "Your father may not be too happy to see us, Dan."

"Oh, I almost forgot," Sue said, with a startled

expression.

"You can both forget it," Dan Ruylander told them. "I'm sure Dad will when he hears the story. He was beginning to regret the whole business anyway. The loss of Kiowa and the Kid will hit him hard, but he can't blame you folks for that. And the men who killed them are dead—or wounded. I don't know which one shot the Kid's horse."

"I'm not sure, Dan, but I think it was Fallon," said Garry.

"You'll be welcome at Rafter," promised Dan Ruylander. "Dirk'll probably insist on paying you for the herd, too."

"Not a chance," Garry Terrell said, with a grin. "I won't accept that much cash, and I can tear up checks as fast as your father writes 'em, Danny."

"Fill 'em up again, bartender," said Dan Ruylander. "I can still taste that gunpowder. Sure takes a lot of liquor to wash it away."

Sue accepted a tiny drink, and clicked glasses with them. "To Rafter and Triangle, Wyoming and Oregon—the dead and the living."

Twenty-Six

The third day out of Rongis they were on the home range, driving along the broad rusty amber plains of the Sweetwater with the eternal gusty winds of Wyoming whipping the dust on the bright October air. The Green Mountains hunched on the south, and the Granites shouldered the northern sky. Rafter was ahead of them, and Dan Ruylander felt his heart rise and his throat tighten with a glad homecoming sensation that set him tingling all over.

They had taken on two new hands in Rongis, and the northeast drive had been smooth and easy over the vast sweeping prairies. Hawk Fallon and Silk Coniff had been buried in the extensive Boothill of John Signor's settlement, among hundreds of other of their kind. Doc Saulteras was caring for the wounded Cahoon and Winslett, and reported that both men would recover. Chill's shoulder was not too serious, but Vern might lose one of his mangled legs.

West of the spread they turned the herd of Durhams and Herefords loose on Rafter land, and went on with the wagons and the remuda. It was a great relief to deliver the herd and be rid of the cattle for the first time in four long months. Dan Ruylander rode his big gray claybank beside the Schuttler wagon, and told Sue Terrell about some of the landmarks she'd see later beyond the ranch. The spectacular pass of Split Rock, in which the trail made three crossings of the Sweetwater, and Independence Rock where Sue's parents had chiseled their names in '51, along with those of thousands of other pioneer emigrants. So many things he wanted to show her, and Dan was excited as a kid.

Then the buildings of Rafter were before them, on a natural terrace above the Sweetwater, and the familiar sight made Dan's eyes smart and his backbone quiver as that rising sensation filled his breast and throat. It wasn't as richly handsome and immaculate as the Terrell's Triangle, but it had a solid rough-hewn beauty of its own. A working ranch, large and prosperous but without much adornment, a living monument to Dirk Ruylander and his family and Jud Crater, and to all the men who had worked and fought and died for them.

The layout looked deserted in the long blue shadows and level sunshine of late afternoon, and Dan knew that most of the men were out on fall roundup, with old Dirk himself at their head this year, in the absence of Jud and Dan and the tophands. The buildings were strongly constructed of timber and adobe brick, the paint fading and flaking on the main structures, the lesser ones weathered to silver-gray. The corrals and sheds were stout and substantial, the gear and grounds in good order.

Old Jesse Worrall, the stable man, and Lydick, a veteran ranch hand, came out of the barn to greet them, eagerly shaking hands with Dan and Jud, Barney and Rusty, and shyly acknowledging introductions to the strangers. "Dirk and the boys are on roundup," Worrall said. "Your sister Judy's gone east to school, and your brother Hudson's in Cheyenne on business. Kinda spoils your homecoming, Danny, but old Dirk'll be in tonight or tomorrow. He's been looking for you every day for weeks."

"We're a little later than we figured on, Jesse," Dan told him.

"Well, you all look as if it done you good," Worrall said. "And I see old Crater ain't lost none of his sourness. But where's the Injun and the Kid, Danny?"

Dan Ruylander told the two old-timers, and it put a blight on this return that Kempter and Antrim would have enjoyed so much.

The wagons parked and unharnessed and the remuda corraled, the riders unsaddled and turned out their mounts to roll in the corral dirt. Then Dan and Jud Crater escorted Sue and Garry Terrell into the big house, while Barney and Rusty Fergus took the other men to the long bunkhouse. Grammaw Hubbard, the white-haired, young-faced housekeeper, welcomed Dan with a resounding kiss and shook hands with Jud and the others. Everybody wanted a bath, and Gram already had the water on heating. She showed the Terrells to their rooms.

Alone in his room with the books, pictures, souvenirs, and knick-knacks that he treasured, Dan Ruylander pulled off his worn through boots and stripped off the filthy sweat-soaked clothing with a sigh of relief. It was disappointing to have the family away, but it was wonderful to be home just the same. And to have Sue Terrell here, in the spacious rambling house he had grown up in.

Dan hung his shell belt and holstered .44 Colt in its old place, and hoped he'd never have to use it again. Except maybe for coyotes, wolves and tin cans, or for hammering fence staples and pounding nails.

Gram Hubbard cooked and served supper, with the help of her silent efficient Indian girl, and it was a most delicious meal.

Later that night, the Terrells having retired, Dan Ruylander and Jud Crater sat in the parlor smoking and chatting with big Barnhorst and Rusty Fergus. A bottle of brandy and glasses stood on the sideboard, and from time to time they rose and helped themselves to another drink. They all found pleasure in being home—for Rafter was really a home to all of them—but there was sorrow in it too, because Kiowa Kempter and Kid Antrim were missing.

Hearing hoofbeats in the night, they filed outside to the gallery and saw Dirk Ruylander and Bo Taverner riding in under the golden harvest moon, and Dan's heart soared once more as he watched his father. They swung down in front of the house as Dan hailed them, and Dirk gripped Dan's hand and pulled him into a brief bearhug of an embrace. Taverner shook hands all around and went off with the horses, while Dirk was greeting Jud and Barney and Rusty.

In the parlor Dirk shed his battered hat and dusty jacket and gun belt, and took the glass of brandy Dan had poured for him. "By God, this is a great night!" said Dirk Ruylander. "Too bad Judy and Hud had to miss it. It's sure good to see you all. But where the hell's young Antrim and the Injun?"

Their eyes told him without words, and Dirk gulped his drink and sank into his favorite leather chair. In the lamplight Dan saw that his father looked older, gaunt and tired, with this new grief etching even deeper lines into his fine strong face. "Well, boys, tell me all about it," Dirk Ruylander said, at last.

For the next two hours, over cigars and brandy, they took turns at reciting the story of their Oregon expedition, with old Dirk shooting pointed questions at them now and then. When it was finished, Dirk sat brooding over the glass in his huge gnarled fist.

"So they're here, Dan," he said, musing aloud. "And they're giving us the herd, because Owen Terrell wanted them to. And you like the boy, and want to marry the girl?"

Dan nodded his cropped tan head. "That's right, Dad."

"Well, I'm not going to stand in your way, Danny," said Dirk, after a strained silence. "Not by a damn sight. You all agree about the Terrells, and you ought to know them pretty well by this time." He smiled with the easy radiant warmth that made people love him. "You young bucks might be wrong, but Jud's never been wrong about women or horses. Except one red-headed gal down in Abilene."

Jud Crater scowled at the general laughter, and Dan said: "So that's why you didn't like Sadie McLain, Jud?"

Crater spat tobacco juice into the fireplace ashes. "Dead ringer for that little bitch wildcat down in Kansas."

After the merriment subsided, Dan glanced soberly at

his father. "So it's all right with you, Dad?"

"Why not, son? It's your life," Dirk Ruylander said. "And with Judy gone this house'll need a young woman, I reckon. We better bed down now, boys. I'm looking forward to meeting our guests in the morning."

Dirk Ruylander sat with Sue and Garry Terrell on the ranchouse veranda, watching the morning sun climb above the Laramie Range and lay lavender shadows on the buffalo grass and sagebrush west of the buildings and the scattered red buttes.

"You favor your father, Garry," he said. "And you look so much like your mother, Sue, it fairly takes my breath away." He showed them the gold locket that held their mother's pictured face. "Well, I'm sure glad it turned out this way."

"We are too, Mr. Ruylander," said Garry Terrell simply.

"I was afraid I'd lost a son, through my own damn stubborn foolishness," Dirk Ruylander murmured. "And now it looks as if maybe I've gained a daughter—and a friend—instead."

"Two friends, at any rate," Sue said, her eyes crinkling as she smiled at him.

"Why not a daughter?"

"Perhaps a daughter—next spring," Sue Terrell said. "I've got to go back home anyway, and I might as well go with Garry. It's better for us to wait and make sure anyway, I think. Next spring, if Dan still wants me, he can come out after me."

"He'll come—if I have to bring him myself," Dirk said, with mock severity. "I ought to ride some of that Oregon Trail before I get too old to sit a saddle."

"Why don't you both come out next spring?" Garry said. "We'd be delighted to have you, and this time Dan could see more of the country."

"We'll see," said Dirk. "If I can't persuade this young lady to stay here now. It's a long ways to Oregon."

Dan came out of the house in time to hear the last sentence. "It's not so far, Dad," he drawled, "If you don't have Silk Coniff on the way out, and three thousand head of cattle on the way back."

"You're going to make the trip again next year then?"

"Looks like I'll have to," Dan Ruylander said. "Sue seems to have her mind set on going home this fall."

Sue Terrell rose and took his big brown hands in hers and stared up at his bronzed features, her smile squinting her blue eyes in that lovely winsome manner. "You're letting me go a little too easy, Dan," she told him. "Oh, I know Jud says give a filly her head. But it's not going to be so simple to get rid of this one as you think, Danny."

"Now where'd you ever get a notion like that, Sue?"

"If you don't come to Oregon after me," she said laughing softly, "I'll come back to Wyoming after *you.*"

"You can't scare me, woman," Dan Ruylander said, smiling down at her shining face with infinite tenderness.

"Rafter's always open to both of you," Dirk Ruylander said. "Consider it your home at time you care to come. Well, Garry, let's saddle up some horses and take a look at this range. I don't think these two will miss us much."

"I guess not," Terrell agreed, laughing. "They never had much chance to be alone together."

"Maybe, with that chance, Dan can change her mind and hold her in Wyoming," said Dirk. "It's going to be a long cold winter."

"Maybe he can, at that," Sue Terrell confessed, with a gay impish smile wrinkling her blue eyes at the corners.

"He'll be trying hard anyway," Dan Ruylander drawled, and they stood with their arms around one another, watching his father and her brother cross the sunny windswept yard toward the corrals of Rafter.

Roe Richmond was born Roaldus Frederick Richmond in Barton, Vermont. Following graduation from the University of Michigan in 1933, Richmond found jobs scarce and turned to writing fiction for the magazine market. These were sports stories and in the 1930s he also played semi-professional baseball and worked as a sports editor on a newspaper. After the Second World War, Richmond turned to Western fiction and his name was frequently showcased on such magazines as *Star Western*, *Dime Western*, and *Max Brand's Western Magazine*. His first Western novel, *Conestoga Cowboy*, was published in 1949. As a Western writer, Richmond's career falls into two periods. In the 1950s, Richmond published ten Western novels and among these are his most notable work, *Mojave Guns* (1952), *Death Rides the Dondrino* (1954), *Wyoming Way* (1958), and in 1961 *The Wild Breed*. Nearly an eighteen-year hiatus followed during which Richmond worked as copy editor and proofreader for a typesetting company. Following his retirement, he resumed writing. Greg Tobin, an editor at Belmont Tower, encouraged Richmond to create the Lash Lashtrow Western series. In these original paperback novels, Richmond was accustomed to go back and rework long stories about Jim Hatfield that he had written for *Texas Rangers* magazine in the 1950s. When Tobin became an editor at Bantam Books, he reprinted most of Richmond's early novels in paperback and a collection of his magazine fiction, *Hang Your Guns High!* (1987). Richmond's Western fiction is notable for his awareness of human sexuality in the lives of his characters and there is a gritty realism to his portraits of frontier life.